Boys
Keep
Being
Born

Boys Keep Being Born

Stories by

Joan Frank

University of Missouri Press

Columbia and London

University of Missouri Press, Columbia, Missouri 65201
Printed and bound in the United States of America

Library of Congress Cataloging-in-Publication Data

Frank, Joan, 1949–
    Boys keep being born : stories / by Joan Frank.
       p.   cm.
    ISBN 0-8262-1355-3 (alk. paper)
    I. Title.
PS3606.R38 B69   2001
813'.54 — dc21   2001045080

㉓™ This paper meets the requirements of the
American National Standard for Permanence of Paper
for Printed Library Materials, Z39.48, 1984.

Text design: Elizabeth K. Young
Jacket design: Susan Ferber
Typesetter: The Composing Room of Michigan, Inc.
Printer and binder: The Maple-Vail Manufacturing Group
Typefaces: Giovanni Book, Frutiger Book

For my cherished mate and witness, Bob Duxbury

◆ ◆ ◆

With loving gratitude to Deborah Mansergh Gardiner

Contents

Acknowledgments

I wish to thank the editors of the following publications, in whose pages some of these stories, in slightly different versions, first appeared: "The Waiting Room" in the *Notre Dame Review;* "The Extraordinary Member of Carlos Artiga" in *Yellow Silk;* "The Queen of Worldly Graces" in the *Kennesaw Review;* "The Scanner" in the *Laurel Review;* "A Stalwart Girl" in *Salmagundi;* "Green Fruit" in the *South Carolina Review;* "The Guardian" in *Faultline;* "When the Universe Was Young" in *Inkwell;* "Boys Keep Being Born" in the *Western Humanities Review;* "What Winter Brings" in the *Bellingham Review;* and "The Sounds That Arrive in the Present" in the *Ohio Review.*

Sincere additional thanks to the editors of *West Wind Review* and *New Millennium Writing.*

"Exquisite," © 1999 by the Antioch Review, Inc., first appeared in the *Antioch Review,* vol. 57, no. 4. Reprinted by permission of the Editors.

"After the Persian" and "Several Voices Out of a Cloud" from *The Blue Estuaries: Poems, 1923–1968,* by Louise Bogan. Copyright © 1968 by Louise Bogan. Copyright renewed 1996 by Ruth Limmer. Reprinted by permission of Farrar, Straus and Giroux, LLC.

I am grateful to Laure-Anne Bosselaar, Karen Brennan, Kurt Brown, Stephen Dobyns, Bob Fogarty, Thaisa Frank, Lynn Freed, Molly Giles, David Kezur, Margot Livesey, Antonya Nelson, Victoria Nelson, Susan Neville, Jack Pelletier, Peter Turchi, Ellen Bryant Voigt, and Chuck Wachtel.

With special gratitude to the MacDowell Colony, the Dorset Colony House, the Barbara Deming Memorial Fund/Money for Women—

and most emphatically and warmly, to Trudy Lewis.

Boys
Keep
Being
Born

Exhibit A

The witness to this story was a woman. Not young, not old. Working a job and buying food and vitamins every week, scanning headlines, sometimes sneaking off to a gentle foreign film like *When Father Was Away on Business*, a plastic orange-juice bottle filled with homemade margarita drink tucked in her purse. She jogged in the park like squadrons of others in her city, an attractive western city near an ocean.

The male lead was a striking fellow, an up-and-coming personage in his city. What is it with these sorts in cities? So many of them! Dashing, earnest, dazzlingly clever. Looking like ads for Polo or Glenfiddich. Boyishly genial, self-ironic, quick; possibly—the inference teases—even wise, though it goes against odds. You see them joshing in clumps outside City Hall after a press conference or on the Opera House steps, or booming and hale in the *comme il faut* restaurants. Groomed all their lives, surely, to exist in just this form for the rest of time: so agile and sparkling no mortal baggage could ever possibly catch them. You gape. You marvel. The impression is these people will never know age or sorrow, though our own memories tell us otherwise. There are *trompes l'oeil*, tricks of the eye, and there are tricks of perception. Like a mirage.

Perhaps then in his early forties—like the other players in this cast—Steven was springy and devil-handsome. Hazelnut hair and gold-flecked brown eyes, a big foamy latte of a man. Let us say he was creative director in a hip young advertising firm, a firm that specialized in clients like Sierra Club and Working Assets, crafting campaigns that popped up in the slickest media, shocking liberal intelligentsia and embarrassing corporate power-blocs. Steven led his brigade like a modest hero: the sort in suspenders and loosened ties whose sleeves seem permanently, *crisply* rolled up; who leans forward at the brainstorming table looking like an Oxford star, hair falling softly, eyes alight with delicious purpose, telling his devoted staff in a high-five call to charge, *Let's do it.* And their young hearts and bodies ripple: Men and women adore his looks, his energy, his ideas. They work hard for Steven for low pay, because it's a legitimate start in this worthy business; because he's fair and warm and lively and funny. They love each other and throw antic parties. They hope it never ends.

Steven and his wife, Marcia—an attorney—also throw wonderful parties. That is important to remember. We'll return to it.

Now, the witness. Jane. Met Steven briefly, randomly, when the philanthropic firm she then worked for threw a rooftop bash in the same city for no less than Mikhail Gorbachev. Honest. There were secret police everywhere and long dark cars moating the block—lots of consulate people; Jane's quirky boss pleased because his generous contributions had obtained him this strike. He personally hoped to open a canful of peace at the center of a circle of influential Russians aboveground and below—media heartthrobs, diplomats, poets—to explode their hearts with cross-cultural affection. In fact these happenings had a *sprung* quality, like those big fat coiled worms the shapes of Chee-tos that come popping out of an unscrewed jar. Anyone who could cadge entry to the affair did, and Steven, who never missed a brilliant event, showed up with a couple of loyal adjuncts, looking gloriously disheveled after a day's strategizing. He exchanged *hellos* with Jane in some unthinking context, perhaps when their two arms made the simultaneous selection of a miniature crab cake off the passing tray. Jane loved those soirees on her office's roof. The blue of evening like a clear, pale wine, the cool saline air, the champagne's delicate snap on the tongue, the way adults lost their daytime dourness with the drink and the hour, and became dangerous and silly. Gorbachev had made his speech right in the middle of the mob—impossible to see him for the heads and TV cams that crowded round at eye level. He called the city "so beautiful, there should be a special tax" on those who lived there. This caused much ironic tittering in his audience about the cost of living they endured. Then the grinning Gorby left, surrounded by tense, black-suited security and scrambling media flacks. In the hubbub Jane and Steven talked, and Jane wasn't immediately thinking anything about it. (These reroutings begin subtly, in life—like a small leak.) His was a pleasant aspect, was all.

Then Steven's agency, called Right Way, returned the diplomacy by inviting Jane's staff to one of its open houses, and Jane had the chance to watch Steven in his domain. Right Way kept offices in one of those fine Boston-brick buildings she'd always admired near the wharf. It was Camelot, certainly. Steven's minions flocked to him; his business colleagues shared that elusive hearty ease among men of comparable stature that translates as territorial respect. (*But how could he afford it*, Jane wondered briefly. Contributions snaked in, but that couldn't be enough. There had to be an Angel—someone anonymously paying bills out of a trust fund, or milking big national grants.) Her frown lifted when she caught sight of her host. Steven was marvelous to watch. He moved at just the right pace. Deft. Eager. Taking leave from each admirer carefully, warmly, fixing each listener with his espresso eyes, pressing their hands in both of his—and it was true: While he spoke to you Steven appeared to care about nothing else in the world so much as what you said, what you felt. His grave attention seemed to cocoon its object in velvet, protect it like cupped treasure.

Let's also be frank. Steven was tall and handsome in the most ridiculously old-fashioned way. Jane began to feel something, as they say.

A quickening.

Of course she knew it was a ruinous idea, and some part of her tried to raise an objection, which other parts of her easily smothered. Oh yes, a bad business; god-awful business, the married man—and common as soda crackers. Living alone a number of years had chipped steadily at Jane, made her feel flinty and reckless. All she could claim to have achieved in the past decade, it had begun to dawn on her, was the avoidance of harm. Sun-

screen, flossing, oil changes. Being prudent. Sameness of routine
had come to feel like an indictment of her own imagination; of
advancing years, even of weekends at *May Fools* and *My Life as a
Dog* and the whole damned *Red/White/Blue* trilogy with her
smuggled plastic bottle of tequila mix. Jane knew better than to
undertake a married man. (She'd stepped in it once or twice as
a pup; fulfilled her disaster quota.) But the city of her era offered
surprisingly few options. All the good men, as the tired saying
went, were gay or girlfriended or, most drearily, married. She'd
grown edgier as her forties arrived, hyperdramatizing the movie
of her life as single people will, the movie nonsingles have no
time to sit all the way through. Too much staring in the mirror
at her questioning face, bale of hair; firm curves—wondering
what on earth it mattered if they were admirable.

Steven asked Jane to lunch one weekday, under pretext of their
two companies' collaborating on a mailing. A Greek place on a
sunny hill, and in her terror Jane arrived early. When he strode
in and she rose and he bussed her quickly on the cheek, she saw
not only that he desired her, but that he was quite content to let
it stand at that: to let the heavy heat between them just sit
there—his eyes knowing; his leg aligning itself with hers at once
under the table, easily, warmly. They chewed at food she later
had no recollection of, some kind of bread and garbanzo paste.
They drank Orvieto, crisp cold white. He paid her compliments.
"You're so beautiful; so wise. Why are you not with someone?"
he murmured after a time and more wine, a barely discernible
smile at the corners of his lovely mouth. Jane's throat closed
then; panicked for words, a zoo creature racing back and forth
with hopeless hunger for what was outside the bars. "There is no
one—" she started simply—how, how to begin? How to frame
it?—opened her hands, and looked sideways toward the floor. It
sounded moronic. One didn't blurt one's pent-upness, one's
shuddering yearning, at a casual lunch. To her horror, frustration
had begun to brim liquid in her eyes. Would she have to *mime*
her message? Jane's mind was pulsing one raw vision: Bed. Deliri-
ous affair. All of modern commerce melting like soft water-

colors down the walls while she and he joined and joined and told funny stories and ate and drank and joined some more. How much sense had this molten coalescing of purpose? When has it ever? Did she have the least rational idea of the beloved? Did anyone? A quality of lost mind it was, certainly, Exhibit A of it—this blast furnace that ignited with a roar and drove us pitilessly, sneeringly, without logic. In a stroke all the building-block concerns—bills, responsibilities, moral clarity—turned to dried insect wings and powdered away. Jane was Anna K., but her Vronsky was not quite stepping up to the plate. What could be the problem? Longing seemed to have petrified the gears of Jane's being, locked it in a tensed, hard grid. Her eyes petitioned: *Please.*

Steven looked back at her evenly. "I love my wife," he said gently. But his leg ran the length of hers, and he had chosen not to move it, and the heat threatened to ignite the cloth that lay between. She'd be glad to stay there with him always then, like that. Never budge from the spot. Be Pompeii figures years hence: *Man and woman in customary mealtime posture, legs aligned.*

After lunch he walked her to her car. It was just turning spring, first buds on trees against a hesitant, fleecy sky. At the top of the hill, the city spread at a distance below them like a fiefdom, and he took her in his arms. Roaring swept Jane's brain and chest and between her legs. She held him by his shoulders and looked up at him, nothing concealing her readiness. Steven gazed at her directly a long time as if trying to find the answer to a private riddle written somewhere on her face, his mouth's corners tensed in what looked like a suppressed wish to smile. Then quickly, thieflike, he pressed his lips to the side of her neck, and she felt it burn; would many years later be able to recall that burn at any time she chose. But when he brought his face back steady with hers his opaque eyes warned and regretted: *I want to, but I cannot. I am not at liberty to.*

Jane stumbled away dazed.

Time passed, of course, and Jane performed her life's chores in a trance of grief. If the mutual wish existed, she told herself

like a baffled tutor, why could it not be granted? And it *had* existed, she knew. He'd held himself just within reach. Withdrawn
as an afterthought. But what was the afterthought's nature? Who
was Marcia, and why was he with her? Steven had said, "I love
my wife," but Jane's caged mind heard it as a ruse. Something
else was at large, she felt, something else being applied. He could
certainly love his wife: that was not the element stopping him.
He wanted to, but. Jane saw behind his face, each time it searched
hers, some sort of curtained argument. She began asking around
town, reading fine print, assembling pieces.

She learned that Steven's job and very existence were all braid-
ed up with his wife's money.

Marcia was a lawyer, a pricey one. He'd met her in Italy. Steven
was from Sydney, Australia (his accent still traceable), a university dropout who'd worked a dozen jobs and was traveling aimlessly, broke. Eldest of a big, scrabbling family whose father
seemed permanently out of work, Steven had no wish to go
home. Marcia was an only child of Los Angeles largesse, reared
in the green manicured hills of Pacific Palisades. She had, quite
simply, never not had what she wanted. She'd struck up with
Steven at a restaurant bar in Fiesole. They'd scampered around
Europe having gymnastic sex—partly from hunger, Steven allowed; partly novelty—though Marcia was not beautiful. Her
face was doughy, her nose pug; her browless eyes distressingly
small; wrong. It was not a face you'd look upon with pleasure,
let alone a second time. But she was cheerful and healthy and
generous; had a fine sexual appetite. They lived well on her vacation money, and on the next-to-last night before the day of
her return flight Marcia had picked up the telephone in their
Bologna hotel room (tall window shutters opening directly out
to a hodgepodge of umber tile rooftops; careening pigeons). She
had said almost parenthetically to Steven—as if suggesting a
restaurant for dinner with the phone already in hand to dial it
up—*Marry me. Come to America with me. I will set you up in the
career you choose.* And he'd thought briefly, and agreed. And who
knows how far beyond that Steven had ever thought.

They came back to the seaside American city and had a small ceremony in Marcia's living room, with a couple of Marcia's friends as witnesses. Marcia resumed her lucrative practice, her partners some of the biggest names in the western United States. She made good on her promise to set Steven up, and Steven chose what he'd always admired, a humanistic, ecology-minded public relations firm that devised ingenious messages and placed them in prominent places to waken the country to its own soilings. It kept the profiteers off-balance. (One famous caption, under a simple photograph that directly helped bring about the "dolphin-safe" laws: *If you saw what it took to collect the tuna for this sandwich, you'd lose your lunch.*) Marcia and Steven found and furnished the wonderful red-brick office, acquired an eager staff, and Marcia tapped connections across the nation as well as in their city for launching her husband. They ate and drank and screwed and hosted, as we have noted, enormous, antic parties, putting up big-name clients and guests from all over the world. Marcia owned a two-story home in a lush neighborhood, the notorious estate in the high upcountry whose name bespeaks wealth, wooded off from the winding highway and with a nighttime view of the entire twinkling city below. They had best foods and wines and good work and plenty of money and each other, and a legion of well-wishers (those proliferating, attractive, clever ones that are a vigorous city's constant product)—subjects of a thriving kingdom, glad to make merry on command.

Steven had no conflicts about the money, though he was fully aware of the irony of its corporate source. It went into the work, you see, and he worked very hard. Why shouldn't he enjoy himself?

"Why shouldn't I enjoy myself? I deserve to live well," he told Jane during one of their after-work drink dates (dinner was too conspicuous, and Steven would not yet come anywhere near Jane's apartment, though not for lack of Jane's urging). They were sitting at a glassed-in bar near the water; outside, pale gold lights of passing ferries and the bridge draped the night. It was fall; a bracing in the air: the city's best time. Jane was watching him the way she usually did; mannerly, pining, stumped: the way a polite tramp might peer through a hofbrau window. She could not cease to desire him, even as he busily steered his little life-beyond-reproach. If he phoned at her office and asked to see her (the context always immaculately offhand), the same quickening squeezed inside her chest, and each time she hoped—like a goose, like a teenager—this time he might accede. *There is no one else—*

But Steven was saying something to her. He was looking out to the lights of evening and saying a trifle sadly, "My marriage is not going to last forever."

Jane stared at him.

"Steven, what are you talking about? You don't just up and say things like that."

He shrugged. "It just won't. I know it," he added quietly, with a quality of voice that Jane couldn't name: an acquiescence. Then he added overbrightly, "Well, marriages don't, usually, do they?"

Generalizations, to divert her.

His features had closed; that careful screen she'd seen earlier. He was not saying it to lend her hope. It had nothing to do with her. He was saying it to himself, and Jane saw she was not in the room with his figurings. His face wore a quiet fatalism, like a defendant reflecting calmly on the verdict of a vengeance-minded jury; eyes trained on an invisible dimension where a crystal ball might have sat. As though he were foreseeing the place and time of his own end.

Jane never went to any of those famous upcountry parties, though once she received an invitation to a surprise birthday party for Steven—Marcia's aides must have found Jane's name on the Right Way mailing list. The invitation had surely gone out to hundreds; filled with gleeful exclamation points—had *chortled*, was the only word for it. Clearly, Marcia was striving to arrange a joyous blowout for her man. Jane had only seen Marcia once during the years of loving Steven. Yes, years of it. But had Jane ever in point of fact loved Steven? The question banged around in her, even years later, like a lost bird. Did she want to go off and live with the fellow somewhere, split the Sunday paper with him, sort his stained undershorts on laundry day? Collude with him in viewing his life story as a myth to be avenged?

Avoid thinking about his encounters with other Janes?

She turned the questions aside. That was not this, she told herself.

What did Jane want? Jane wanted to melt into meaning. Be subsumed into it. Have and hold and mean. Really, it wasn't complicated. Remember the look that shot between Warren Beatty and Faye Dunaway just before the sheriff's posse blasted them in *Bonnie and Clyde*? They knew it was their last living moment. And their eyes telegraphed to each other, in one beat, the most thrilling understanding. A *hail and farewell* of purest intimacy, a clean-through knowing. Two parts of a single thing, that look. Nothing to do with *couture* or witty words or how much anybody weighed.

That was what Jane wanted.

Of course, you had to separate that look from all the murder stuff.

Jane lifted trapped spiders out of the tub on a little hammock of toilet tissue, setting them free out the window before she turned on the shower. She wrote a check to any kid who rang the doorbell with a plastic janitor-tote full of bad candy or horrible snot-colored candles. She pulled the car over to hear *Finlandia*, turned way up to reverberate in her bones—listened as if with a stethoscope to the tender message in Dvořak's *New World* theme. Her birthday wish had always been the same since she could remember—pausing flushed and momentous before six, seven, eight candles, before ironic, forbearing faces of parents, of cake-lusting children: *Please let everyone and everything everywhere have happiness forever.* In those days she would sit on the porch steps at dusk in her sunsuit and sandals, arms twined loosely between her knees, considering with calm pleasure the fact that someone, that absolutely same exact minute, was growing up somewhere far away who would love her.

No, Jane had glimpsed Marcia only once. And the vision, like the burning imprint of Steven's mouth along the side of her neck, was something she would always carry.

Marcia had been strolling with her husband.

Jane had driven herself to the red-brick complex containing Steven's office in one of her lonely acts of street-where-you-live self-torment. A five-year anniversary celebration for Right Way was in progress, as Jane had known it would be, and the entire complex was participating: Outfits with linked sympathies had set up display tables piled with brochures and demonstrations and sales offers (massage, kayaking, chutneys, windchimes, birdhouses, telescopes, camping tents) lined up along the open arcade. People milled and wandered, eating popcorn with yeast sprinkled on it, drinking fresh-pressed apple juice; a pleasant river of voices and celestial ping-pang of stirring chimes. Jane's eyes, in the ageless reflex of obsession, both hoped and dreaded to locate her beloved, sore to catch sight of him as she poked around, and after a time of walking and looking listlessly at the bland enthusiasms of the merchants and customers—*the ease of these people! the legitimacy they enjoyed; assured, settled; their comfortable right to time and space*—at last she did see him. At some distance down the corridor, between giant potted palms, she spotted him walking—then at once saw his wife beside him. Marcia was dressed in a dark navy suit. She must have come from her own office. *Nailing the last nails into her final arguments, into some luckless bastard's coffin,* Jane thought. She backed into a group surrounding a gyroscope display; flashing silver spheres with slender axles, teetering as they spun along a taut string—and peered again as discreetly as she could. That was when Jane saw that Marcia was rather painfully not beautiful. Saw the stolid body, too heavy up top and too thin in the legs—the odd, monkeyish face. But in the next blink Jane saw Marcia's arm linked tightly through Steven's, clasping his forearm as they walked; her other hand reached over to secure his arm in enthusiastic two-handed pressure. Marcia was looking into Steven's face, perhaps saying a few words.

Jane could never, recalling that moment, shake the memory of Marcia's face.

Marcia's face had looked into her husband's with tender light and a kind of—imploring question. Marcia's eyes said, *My dearest, is this not exactly what you have wanted? Have we not sown well and reaped a bounty? Exactly as you wished?*

Marcia's eyes said, *It's good, then, isn't it? Won't you tell me it's good?*

Steven's eyes, which had glanced perhaps once, perfunctorily, at his loving wife's as if scarcely able to remember her—were busy scanning randomly, restlessly, patrolling some internal tension as if casing the area for terrorist bombs. Then his eyes caught Jane's. He made not a flicker of acknowledgment; held her gaze one ferocious beat—then clicked his gaze's trajectory a quarter-turn forward at measured, leisurely speed: straight ahead of his path. The message was explicit: *Do not. Do not. Do not.*

Jane would not. Dared not. Would never have. She waited a few minutes until the couple was past, then made her way out of the complex in the opposite direction, wishing with all her power that she might be purged of mind, might belong seamlessly to the murmuring, puttering crowd.

Now we return to the parties Marcia and Steven threw, turning guests into houseguests, especially Steven's clients. One couple spending a great deal of guest time at the upcountry mansion were Kate and Everett Austin. Both were young, a bit surly and a bit plump, as if the baby fat hadn't yet been siphoned off nor adult courtesies instilled. Kate had made herself a national name in her war against the use of sugar in infant formula sent with third-world food drops. Incendiary articles, highly publicized visits, her own press conferences: Kate was quick and effective, like a chemical gas, when she worked. She traveled a lot, and Jane, who knew of Kate by name, had never known Kate had a husband until she was introduced to them at one of Right Way's happy-hour open houses. He looked like a surfer: nodded a smileless greeting—eyes widening for acknowledgment— plainly dubious of this crowd, these gestures, of most social transactions anywhere. Jane briefly felt chastised by this unfriendly honesty, for her complicity in the ritual of being intro-

duced at a cocktail hour. Steven mentioned that the young couple was staying with him and Marcia. He had greatest respect for
Kate's work; was about to design a media campaign to assist her
upcoming fact-finding tour in West Africa. In fact there was talk
of filming a documentary for public television. And the funding?
Who else, Jane thought drily. Marcia would find delightful anyone Steven found delightful, and funding would naturally follow. Jane brushed ineffectively at the images repeating in her
mind's video, sprightly and interminable as an infomercial: The
four having animated breakfast in thick terry robes, every luxu-
ry at hand—bagels, waffles, the *Times* flown in that morning,
the homemade preserves and fresh-squeezed juice, a big, light-
drenched kitchen with its customized island in the middle,
capped by the dense woodblock table at which they laughed and
took more butter, thanks—carrying their fragrant heavy mugs of
dark roast out to the redwood deck in misted sunlight, leaning
at the sturdy sun-warmed railing, breathing eucalyptus coolness,
last morning fog wisps licking at the long green leaves, survey-
ing the sheltered kingdom out to its westernmost edges. Across
the ocean lay Asia and all the archipelagoes and blue mysteries
of the Pacific.

All of it was theirs while they looked.

When Jane next phoned Steven's office extension, hoping to
coax him to a drink or bite to eat—perhaps to reassure herself
of his patterns—the answering voice was Kate's.

"Right Way," said the female voice, disinterestedly.

Steven usually answered his own phone.

"Um—hello? Is Steven around?"

"He's away for a little," said the female. "This is Kate. Can I
take a message?" The question was routine, but Jane paused.
Kate's voice was entirely void of the inflection so automatic to
Americans answering telephones, especially women: that bright,
upward lilt whose tone and modulation signal the caller, *I long
to be a pure conveyance of your will.* With a sickening start, Jane recognized this latter tone to be true of herself. Her telephone voice
raced ahead of people in the road, clearing away large sticks and
rocks, strewing scented petals.

Kate's flat voice had said only, *I am here. And cannot wait not to be.*

It had no time for any Other. Perhaps this near-rude lack of affect cut through obsequiousness and lechery in corporate boardrooms and African airports alike.

And Jane had declined to leave word, thinking it odd that the famous Kate Austin would be answering office phones. Yet she knew the place was always shorthanded. Steven was probably working on the West Africa project there with her, or stopping through while chauffeuring the four of them (in his spanking-new sport-utility vehicle) on some jolly day trip. Maybe, Jane thought, the four were to rendezvous that evening at a restaurant. Jane remembered the glimpses she'd got of Kate at the open house. She had limp, amber-colored hair and a rather chipmunk-cheeked face. Her clothes—jeans and hooded sweatshirts that zipped up the front—strained round her upper arms and middle and thighs. A tomboy who still forgot herself at meals. Jane had watched Steven work the room somewhat nervously the night of that gathering, often glancing back to see that Kate and her husband had what they needed. He seemed to be in a certain amount of transparent thrall to the larger names, Jane noticed with irritation. It was as if he had never been substantial enough in himself to stand for anything, so that he became startled and fawning when he was near those who actually did. It was easier—safer—to stand behind them, be a kind of livery to them, back a few notches from the action. This stance could be called respect. It was more, Jane realized, a kind of fear.

In the midst of those many following months of quick drinks, rarer lunches, clipped phone exchanges in which Jane inevitably came just short of begging Steven, there came one awful night. One awful night when Marcia left town to visit her mother, and Steven phoned Jane and for the first time consented to come to her apartment. She'd done everything possible to make it easy: food and drink, the place spotless, plants watered, the little sound system loaded with Catalan guitar. She wore a silk top and jeans, had freshly shampooed hair giving off an apple blossom scent she'd loved since childhood. She waited in silence, perched erect at the edge of her studio couch, got up and walked, fingers interlaced and squeezing, sat again. The hour of meeting passed. He phoned; he would be late. She sat, walked, sat, and the postponed hour passed. Jane wanted to scratch at her arms 'til they were streaked white with scraped skin. She put the food away and was about to leave the apartment to pace the street when he phoned once more and stammered at her; not making sense. Bereft, maddened, she yelled at him.

"What the hell are you trying to do?"

"I'm afraid," he shouted back. "I'll come," he added hastily.

When the buzzer at last sounded, electrifying her arms and legs with prickling adrenaline, she pattered double-time in bare feet down the old-smelling stairwell, taking him by the hand to lead him up. At once she was struck how out of place his handsome being looked there. *This was not a man for old smelly stairwells,* and a moment's shame flashed through her. Then he disappeared into the bathroom, and when he emerged, she was handing him a glass of cold Orvieto, in honor of their first meeting, where first she had known *He is my desire.*

And then it happened again, the way it had by the parked car near the Greek restaurant. They slid to the floor, him above her, looking into her face, the corners of his mouth flickering. Again she saw him trying to read a signal, an instruction, somewhere on her face. And though all her eyes could transmit was *Yes please yes,* that was not the message he sought. At length he rose and pulled her to her feet.

"I am leaving," he said. "And I want you to be all right with that."

Jane could not look at him. She felt stripped of skin.

He took her chin and tilted it up so she had to see him.

"A smile now," he said.

She stared at him. "How can you. How can you."

He looked away quickly and his voice grew rough. "To see, perhaps, if I still can. To see if someone would still want me to."

Jane stood stupidly in her living room, listening to his shoes finding their way down the darkened stairwell. She heard the door clump shut, the car start outside, heard its gears engage and engine hum as it sped down the street and beyond hearing.

Now pour in some time. Time intervening like cool milk. Days and weeks and months, smoothing, washing. In that flowing mercy of time, Jane allowed routine to carry her, obeying the edicts of women's magazines and folk wisdom. She drove up to visit her sister's family in the mountains, swam miles of laps with stabbing strokes at the municipal pool, brought a musical plush toy (a smiling otter that played "La Vie en Rose") to the friends across the bay who'd just had a baby. She made the margaritas extra strong to weep hard in *Cinema Paradiso* and *Il Postino*, emerging from theaters in the dark so people would not observe her swollen face.

In time, in heedlessly constant, pouring time, Jane began to allow the fact of Steven to drift. Her boss continued to throw rooftop happenings, lately for Richard Gere and the Dalai Lama. She found a cozy gym and a good cheap Taiwanese place and an excellent used CD store, where they had all the Glenn Gould versions of Bach's English and French Suites.

The point had arrived when Jane forgot to remember she was sad. And that, of course, is when the phone call from Steven came.

His voice was breathy, bearing down. It sounded ruined, and in fact he was.

He was leaving the country.

He asked her to meet him.

Jane was amazed to notice that she felt no immediate squeeze. Instead—a queer curiosity. Yes. She would see him.

He met her at the front door of a flat in a splintery Victorian on the edge of town. Right Way had left the stately Boston bricks, had set up at this rented flat. Two people worked for Right Way now: Steven and a pregnant niece. Soon it would be only the pregnant niece, and then Right Way would quietly fold. The room behind him was lit by tubes of weak fluorescent light, the way Jane imagined a police interrogation cell. Filled with stacks of dusty boxes of files and papers. One gunmetal, army-barracks desk and two folding chairs of similar metal. The desk was covered with papers; there was a feverish smell of old paper and sweat in the room.

He embraced Jane at the door and tried to kiss her wetly on the mouth. Jane ducked around him and entered the room. Steven looked wrongly put together, as if a child had misman-aged Mr. Potato Head and stuck legs where ears should be. He turned and again lunged for her from behind, wrapping her, try-ing to run his hands over her breasts. Again she twisted away. She had never known him like this.

"Steven. What happened."

He stopped still a moment as if someone had snapped fingers in front of his eyes; sat heavily at the littered desk, gestured her to one of the folding chairs. He seemed to have no shoulders, sit-ting as though someone had just snuck up behind him and yanked out his spinal column in one slick upward flourish.

She could have figured it out, she later realized, if she'd thought about it just a little harder.

Steven had fallen in love, or believed he had, with Kate Austin. *(But she's dowdy!)* Commenced the affair three years ago in his and Marcia's home with everybody in it. *(On the living room couch? The laundry room floor in the basement? Moonlight through the window? Straining to be quiet, not to wake the other two? Oh, God.)*

Kate had consented at the outset—it seemed she had little allegiance to the surfer—but as Steven's ardor grew, perhaps because Kate was the single thing he could not easily have, he began to prevail dramatically on her. He wanted them both to divorce so they could marry each other. Kate found this ex-treme—her allegiance to anyone apparently mild—and drew back from him. This fired Steven's obsession, and he began to neglect his work and draw heavily on his bank account to seek her out, beg, and threaten her. Phoned her at every hour, flew to wherever she was, cruised the Austin house in New Mexico, raged, cajoled, wept; made scenes, ultimatums. Kate finally went to the police and obtained a three-state court injunction against Steven, stipulating severest penalties for his making any word or gesture toward her. Then she and the surfer moved to Montana.

Prior to the injunctions, while still gripped by the belief that he could marry the cool, indifferent object of his desire, Steven had confessed to Marcia. She threw him out at once, pulled the plug on Right Way's offices and payroll, on every facility and contact propping Steven—but not before she made him know the fullness her wrath. Jane did not ask for particulars—did not want to hear the pictures and sounds that would embed in her mental archives. Marcia was granted one of the swiftest divorces on the county's record (no word of it in the papers), and Steven would claim absolutely nothing of their collective estate, except one thing.

A one-way international air ticket.

He was returning to Australia. Some friend of a friend, reached in Sydney by phone, had agreed to give him a temporary job driving a magazine delivery van.

It was enough. Jane rose. Steven leapt from his chair and came over to clasp her; trying yet again to grope and tongue her. He smelled beery. It was repulsive, and she wrenched from him with a disgusted cry.

"Steven! Why this? Why now?"

He stared at her, groggy and dim, like a drunk apprehended in the feral greed of shoveling food into his mouth, and somehow it frightened Jane to see him not even try make of it other than what it was.

"I thought that—since there was nothing stopping us," he said, his voice low with its own foulness.

Jane blinked. All those months, years. Spinning her patient bewildered fantasies; equal parts Rogers and Hammerstein and Boris Pasternak. And now to think of him as the unsavory perv. The thing to be *got rid of* by no less than legal injunction. Gross, unbalanced; elicitor of scorn and loathing.

Something you scraped off your shoe.

She craned to assemble the fast-forward history, trying to fit it to the man she beheld. His clothes looked slept-in, his jaws smeared with stubble, eyelids heavy. He was sleeping in a rented shack on someone's property, someone who'd pitied him, letting him use the space until the morning he would catch his plane. And he *was* pitiable. The city-star who'd moved so winningly among his costars, whose words and actions had embodied a nearly balletic grace. Part of Jane felt genuinely sad for this once-and-ne'ermore king, who'd taken the world and overturned it upon his own head like a bowl of slimy porridge.

She stared at Steven. The fact that her early desire could as easily have brought him to this, registered faintly then—blotting itself against her awareness damply but purposefully, like lipsticked lips. He had chosen the famous, dowdy one—yet the retribution would have been the same had he chosen her. Retribution playing out now, before her eyes.

Weirdly, accidentally—unjustly, perhaps—she'd been spared.

"I am leaving," she said, stepping through the door of the flat.

He stood quite still, his face slack. She paused halfway through, turning to gaze back at him.

"And I want you to be all right with that."

It would be years before Jane would come to feel this story taking its place under the overgrowth of other stories. Years before she'd see her part in it as neither mere nor important—instead, she has thought, maybe more like that of a tree. Yes. A rather attractive tree, say, at the periphery. A tree that watched it all. Except that this tree also became part of the story. Stepped in from its spectator position at the border, walked and talked, acted, reacted—and remembered. Which we don't know that actual trees ever do, exactly; at least, not in the same way.

The Waiting Room

Rita Carr came to Paris when her marriage of fourteen years had ended and with it, her job.

It was a long-term mistake, she liked to say, and there was nothing for it now but to begin again, if you can call it beginning when you're a little past the middle, she thought—when you are forty-six. Saying the number aloud, in a voice that quavered only slightly, she thought herself decisive, and daring. People dodged having to say the numbers now, she noticed, because in spite of everyone knowing better, the advanced number was like an embarrassing score, or a statement of the progression of a virulent disease.

Rita could say the number if she was asked, which happened sort of obliquely. She would be asked it in roundabout ways by women she invited to lunch, women she had hoped to develop as friends. But when she obliged their directness with her daring honesty it seemed to discomfit them—they looked around the room and spoke quickly of other matters, and tended not to initiate engagements after that unless she prodded and dogged them. She would feel a bit chaotic, uncertain how she'd offended, then decide it was her imagination, and put that woman's name on her list of must-see's. Rita was tall, had pale skin, faint red eyebrows, and slightly protruding, pale blue eyeballs; one of those female faces that seem a blank slate before makeup—a face that if she made it up properly and had a decent amount of sleep and not eaten too much candy the day before, could look actually pretty, pretty in that almost-model way you see of women out to dinner, in restaurants with velvet on the walls. Untended, Rita's rinsed-auburn hair seemed to sit too far back on her scalp, like a mannequin's slipped wig. But with a good haircut and the right moisturizer and a pleasant, indirect light, and

of course some serious organizing of clothes and belts and cos-
tume jewelry, she could look almost mysteriously desirable. It
was hard work. Rita had big feet, and a gap between her two front
teeth.

The man to whom Rita had been married, a doughy, balding
fellow with the habit of working a toothpick around one side of
his mouth, had finally agreed to buy out her half of the little radio station. The marriage, she later told me, was something she
had done the way many people undertake marriage, for lack at
the time of anything better to do. Rita took a temp job as a receptionist for a winery in the Napa Valley, and when the local
college advertised a Paris semester, she gathered up her buyout
money and signed on, with the idea she might purvey her experience with the vineyards and never come back to America.

Rita had no French. It was the first trip she had taken in the
fourteen years since she'd married. The program set her up in a
dorm room in the fourteenth district, near the Place d'Italie. It
was a pleasant enough neighborhood, wide streets lined with
blank-faced apartment blocks, the métro stop bubbling up a
steady stream of students and housewives and commuters like
an underground spring. But the problem of language at first
exhausted Rita, and for a few days she felt heavy and slept a
lot, rarely leaving the dorm. Every time she set foot outside the
building—a great, glassed-in affair with enormous tour buses
crouched out front, farting black exhaust straight into the doors
and windows—just to buy a sandwich, or a bottle of wine or a
sack of cookies meant a terrible struggle, and her face would
flame as she fought to concentrate on counting out the right
number of francs for the bitterly contemptuous clerks at the
checkout counters. All they had to hear was a single *je voudrais*
in her Oklahoma drawl, the r's round and slurry, to press their
lips into a bloodless line and turn away as if she'd never been
standing there. She relied for a while on the dorm's cafeteria,
where the personnel (young French students, one eye on their
open textbooks as they doled up overcooked cauliflower) had at
least a flickering comprehension of English and a longer toler-

ance for her twangy American stammer. It was colder that winter than anything she had felt for a long time; snowing on and off in paperweight swirls. She often sat for hours in the dorm's foyer, writing carefully chipper postcards to people she did not miss, drinking expensive coffees.

Rita tried for a time to befriend the other students in her program. They were mostly women of eighteen and nineteen, daughters of retired aerospace workers with neat tract homes nestled in green suburbs; daughters whose trust funds stipulated that certain checks might be cut before the age of maturity, but only for educational endeavors. These were big-boned, big-breasted girls who spent every day making up carefully and blow-drying before heading out to St. Michel and the Opéra to shop and shop and shop. They seemed to have decided the best way to make themselves felt in the city was to strike bored-princess poses: complaining to Rita about being heckled in the métro stops and streets; feigning insouciance about the great roaring Gothic majesty and filth and impossible centuries of dripping history around them—"It's only a city," one had sniffed. In fact on arrival the young women had become briskly practical, mastering their awe as well as the métro system, shifting into a cool-huntress determination, a singleness of purpose that might be read on their faces if one looked twice: to get a French lover. The girls were polite to Rita, but they always seemed to find reasons to be unable to meet her for dinner or a drink or a walk. Rita had a creeping, rancid sense, watching them look nervously past her in the dorm lobby or along the adjacent Boulevard St. Jacques (where Americans could spot one another from blocks away by their strapping size, the fulsome flesh on their bones)—that the young women felt that to be seen standing near her would spoil their image, and their luck.

Rita enrolled in the college's French instruction, but it was taught by an old woman whose eyes swam like trapped fish behind her thick lenses. Madame Bergeron—while very sweet—never appeared quite sure what was supposed to happen next; it was like crawling through narrow tunnels to try to apply the half-

wit phraseology of Madame's lessons to the furious world of
Parisian vernacular. The speech of daily transactions seemed to
whip past Rita like the thin roar of the TGVs, the *grande vitesse*
trains that streamed over the countryside. Rita had glimpsed
these bullet-shaped trains sitting in rows, in the big echoey stations, and thought about them—at night, in her skinny bunk
bed, the streetlight a milky cataract through the dirty window
glass. She even fancied her tiny dorm room was shaped like a
train's sleeping car. One day, because she had money for it, because the guidebooks called it pleasant and because it was rela-
tively near, she bought a ticket to Orléans.

I was surprised at how sorry I felt for Rita just after this event,
and unaccountably, how repelled; I had an idea then what had
occurred with her lunch partners. I was teaching with another
college housed in the dorm that winter, and she had cornered
me one morning in the coffee bar, presumably because I was an
American, a woman closer to her in age, and—I am sure she
hoped—in sympathies. But I was overloaded that semester with
too much grading, and too little unstructured time in the city
(perhaps the only time I have been relieved to float the truth of
that situation as an excuse). I apologized that I'd rarely have a
free moment; thus, the reports she began to offer of what followed, necessarily came in the form of short summations.

It began with the trip to Orléans.

It was late February, freezing, and the sky and land seemed sat-
urated with the grays of the millennia of winters that had gone
before. Mist covered the country, but Rita made herself study the
outlines of suburbs and farmhouses gliding past, congratulating
herself for her decisiveness. Orléans, it turned out, was a not un-
pleasant town, with its requisite tourism office, its Peruvian musicians on the station steps—but a town that declared itself and
was over, for her distracted purposes, too quickly. She walked to
the cathedral—stone interior emanating currents of stunningly
cold breath; a crypt must be warmer, she thought—to the various statues of Jeanne d'Arc, with their florid inscriptions, to the
art gallery, which by comparison with the Disneyland bedlam of

the Louvre, seemed unnervingly empty on a weekday afternoon. She watched yuppie wives pushing babies in expensive strollers, students languishing in billows of their own smoky exhalations, elderly women squinting at the market-stall vegetables. She wandered the *centre ville,* with its concentric circles of wealth— Gucci and St. Laurent outlets at center, Monoprix and shabbier brasseries on the next orbiting ring, little Asian cafés next, and so on. And suddenly there was nothing left to do in Orléans, unless she waited for a matinee.

Rita's face and words reflected a constant, slow astonishment —even in retrospect—as she told me about standing on the track, unable to make out the blurred, nasal announcements of departing trains, her stomach fluttering as she stepped onto what she was in no way sure was the right train. And as soon as it pulled out and was gaining smooth speed, she stammered her question to a bored-looking kid reading a computer magazine, and at his disgusted response her stomach completed its fall. She was heading the wrong way, further out into the country, and now she would have to wait and renegotiate a return to Paris from the next stop. It was so hard, so hard. Her head hurt and her eyes ached. She had plopped down opposite the curt young man, leaned her head back against the blue Naugahyde, and in the process of closing her eyes saw the conductor emerging at the other end of the car.

He was a young man, perhaps in his early thirties, and even in her exhaustion she had no trouble noticing he was good-looking. Of medium height, dark eyes—Italianate, the way velvet pupil and iris meshed—and soft brown hair set off by the navy of his uniform and cap. (Why did Frenchmen always have such good hair?) He noticed her at once, and also at once seemed alarmed by his own straying gaze: before it could embarrass him he had yanked it away and was steering it along its professional rounds—but it kept escaping and flitting back at her, for fractions of instants. *Messieurs-dames,* he murmured, and people went about their bored proffering of paper, and he about his punching and inspecting, in the dignified and weary movements that seem to tie French lives together like connect-the-dots draw-ings: war, love, death, birth; heroism, treachery—all first requir-ing proper tickets, proper validation.

The two kept wary track of each other as he made his way through the car, and when he stopped at her side she became aware she felt short of breath. When she looked up at approxi-mately the moment he stood next to her, she fancied she saw ea-gerness, shyness, and a certain amusement jostling for position upon those handsome features.

"You have problem," he said in English.

"Yes," she said, coloring. She tried, in pained French, to de-scribe her mistake, but he cut her off. "*Bon:* I tell you. You go when I say." And at the first stop he appeared, nodding to her and motioning her to follow him down from the car. Slicing sideways through the commuters in raincoats huddled around the yellow departures display, he made emphatic motions at the line naming the next express for Paris. He pointed as if to un-derscore its platform number, and looked hard at her. "*C'est noté?*" he demanded, touching his own eye, and jerking his head toward the billboard display, as if he were drilling a vexingly slow pupil for an exam and her grade was to directly reflect on his honor. "You see?"

She saw. She caught her train, but not before she had given Alain Lemieux her dorm's address and telephone and learned that he lived in Reims, in an apartment loaned to employees of the railroad, while he looked for permanent housing. He was separated, he said, with no telephone, and he worked rotating shifts. But he would call her.

When Rita told me this story I managed to hide an immedi-ate sense of dread; what Americans call (looking meaningfully at you) *a bad feeling*. Who has not, by now, listened to some poor creature rattle on like the marked animal you already see her to be, and who has not tried, against fierce instinct, to persuade oneself of one's own overbright reassurances? Occasionally it ap-pears we are given the task of simply sitting out the trajectories of people's emergencies, just so we can attend the inevitable call—like ambulances parked around the block: playing cards, eating sandwiches.

Rita had to walk carefully home through the icy gray that day (for the streets were slippery) with her slow and agitated thoughts, her plans to change everything. The list scrolled before her: a new outfit, a better coiffure; she could splurge for a tiny vial of real French perfume; perhaps even join that health club with the fake beach, where all her young costudents went to preen. And as she plotted and assembled her arsenal of persuasions, she waited for Alain's call.

It came in three days. Lurching over their words, they arranged to meet the following Saturday at the Luxembourg Gardens; they would walk to rue Vavin for coffee. The day was, as usual, freezing; all color leached from the close sky, the squat shrubs waiting. Alain stood by the fountain, which was empty and still; one leg propped up on its rim. He wore a collared cotton shirt, thick woolen vest, trousers in the current safari fashion, and a leather jacket. He looked like an ad in *Esquire*.

"I can't tell you how nice he was," Rita breathed a few days later, as we walked back to the dorm from the métro. We had recognized each other amid the bodies pushing through the exit turnstiles into the cold daylight. When we were free of the crush, making our way along St. Jacques in the waning afternoon, I questioned her about her first encounter with the young conductor.

"He treated me . . . " She studied the sidewalk, placing her big feet in an odd, tentative gait I had begun to recognize. "—with this incredible *delicacy*. So polite." She paused again. "Like I was made of glass and jewels."

Of course he did. I asked her what she had learned about him this time.

"Well. We were sitting on these stools, in a bar on the rue Vavin, and got coffees, and he told me—best he could, you know; his English is as rotten as my French," she gave a little *har* of a laugh, and a glassy grin. "—told me he was trying to find an apartment. He said he'd been married, but that that was over. He didn't seem to want to say much about it," her voice trailed. Alain was curious about Rita's history; asked repeatedly about California. "He said he would like to see me again," she added, glancing sideways at me.

The two had wandered rue Vavin, peering into fragrance shops and baby clothiers, chocolatiers, and picture framers; startled through the window glass by the clerks' thin, even stares, as if the Paris shopkeepers had been dreaming something pleasant until that moment. It was too cold to stay long on the street; Alain said goodbye to her at the Montparnasse stop—this time, he took her hand. He would have to catch a métro to the Gare, and an evening train to Reims. It all seemed too short for Rita; more so since she wasn't sure when their next date would be. Alain was to phone her at the dorm before the week was out. It seemed the train people kept switching his schedules, so he rarely knew in advance when he'd be free. She'd offered several times to phone him at a predesignated spot, but he'd insisted it was not possible. Rita would wait for his call.

She looked at me. "I've already told myself, whatever it turns out to be, I'll just be glad if I can call him a friend." She waited.

I didn't hesitate. "Sure. Certainly. That's the way." In the early stages of these events we have no difficulty believing that we'll be fine with that—that anyone would have no trouble being fine with that.

Two weeks later I found a note from Rita in my dormitory mail, asking me for help composing a letter in French. I rang her room, and agreed to meet her at the coffee bar downstairs. I must explain that my French is never what I wish, but it does bring me the satisfaction of tossing out little mouthfuls of perfunctory phrases like sparkle. As I left my room, I picked up my *Larousse de Poche* and some paper and seated myself at one of the circular tables amid the rattling dishware and steaming espresso machines; as usual, the young Algerian bartender had turned the rock music up to deafening. Rita appeared after a few minutes. She must have scrubbed her face, for it wore a sheen, perhaps of moisturizer, or those expensive pearlescent lotions women buy. I could detect a too-sweet floral scent. Her eyes were large and her smile enormous, almost goofy, and again I felt that queer combination of sympathy, the wish to reassure her, with a vague distaste, a wish to run away. The young women students eyed us as they passed our table, some in fancy trench coats their mothers had bought them, others in cutoff overalls, flight jackets, and hillbilly work boots, thatches of dyed-strawberry hair flopping into their eyes—and in my increasingly odd role as matron-lecturer turned scribe, I nodded them meaningfully along.

"Now then," I turned to Rita. "What's happened."

Rita's eyes bulged. As their second date, she and Alain had chosen to meet in Vincennes, the pricey suburb just north of the city, where the large *hôtels particulières* as well as the streets and public squares were named for war generals. Another dirty-ice-colored day. They walked the Parc Floral, but it was so cold, they had to imagine the flowers. Finally they gave up on the outdoors and retreated to a brasserie near the métro; they ordered hot brandies. As the liquor warmed them, Rita grew dreamy, and as if he'd ascertained it, Alain chose that exact moment to tell her, working his face in an odd way: *I have three secrets.*

"What on *earth*," I demanded.

Rita took a breath, and stared into some hidden dimension between us. "He has a child," she began. I made no reaction, and truthfully felt not a morsel of surprise. "A daughter," she went on, looking steadily into the mystery-zone on the tabletop—by the woman he had been married to. Perhaps the girl was ten; Rita wasn't sure she had heard the age correctly. He sees the child once in a while, Alain told Rita.

"That's one," I said.

There was a pause.

"He had a girlfriend for a long time, who hates his wife and does not get along well with the daughter," Rita spoke carefully, the way she placed her feet when she walked. "They had a terrible relationship. They screamed at each other, threw things, drove past each other's apartments in the middle of the night to see who might be there—things like that," she said. She kept looking into the air above the table, as if describing tiny holographic scenes gesturing there, visible only to her. "He says he is very glad to be out of it. Well, at least I think he tried to say that," she glanced at me, colored a moment, looked off again.

"That's two," I said.

She looked blank suddenly. "I'm not sure we ever talked about a third," and her voice trailed off again. She seemed to have lost track of the verve and purpose with which she'd sat down—as if these qualities were a frequency, and her tuning gear had wavered, unable to lock on.

"What are you going to do next," I said.

She shifted slightly in her chair. Both of us had forgotten to fetch coffees. She craned her neck around to look behind her at the noisy espresso bar, then at me, then back into that mysterious dimension on the tabletop.

"I offered to go out to Reims for a day, if he would meet me there," she said. "Alain said to wait and see what his schedule would be. He's going to call," she added rapidly, with that peculiar admixture in her voice of sudden bravado, reassurance, and trailing-off. Listening to Rita had the effect of making me begin to feel vague and uncertain, as if perhaps I had imagined much of my own personal history; as if we were both fading systematically into the noisy air. I squared myself and sat up taller, leaning toward her a little to stretch my spine.

"Rita, what do want from this?" I said it quietly.

She looked at the table. Her eyes had dulled some, yet her voice kept the careful modulations of a coffee shop hostess.

"I want to tell him that he doesn't have to worry if he just wants to be friends. I mean he's so nice and all, and—I would be very happy just to be friends with him and—respect him as a friend, and—maybe we can still keep something up after I have to go back to the states . . . " She looked at me.

"That's what you want me to write in French for you?"

She nodded, coloring in mottled patches. "I just can't say it right," she said, "and I can never think fast enough to say it when I'm with him." She didn't have Alain's address, but she could hand the letter to him when they next met. Rita had tried to improve her French during classes. She had even hired a private tutor recommended by Madame, a plump woman who also worked at the dorm's switchboard. They would sit opposite each other here in the coffee bar, and Rita would *écouter* and *répéter* until her head rang and throbbed.

She frowned.

"I thought I would try to stay in France. If I could get a job in Épernay, near Reims, where the champagne cellars are—I'm going to start asking around, you know?" Her eyes fixed suddenly on mine. She seemed to hope I would finish her sentences for her, and in doing so, shoehorn her into these designs. Again I was repelled. Was it that Rita somehow embodied, at forty-six, what the rest of us work so hard to contain, or stave off, or simply deny? It was nearly unbearable to watch her—cut free and floating, tumbling and dying in deep space. My skin itched. But I heard myself urging Rita on in her ballooning, dream-cloud notions, telling her there was no reason why she should not branch out, check around, see what was available—every cliché that might appease, that might help ease me away. She listened with that air she had of hearing something else at the same time; something hard to make out. I squeezed her shoulder as I rose from the table, and almost in penance for racing away—like putting my hasty signature to a bill—agreed we should have dinner soon.

That evening, I sat down at the formica desk. Beneath the whey-thin fluorescent light, I wrote in French: *Dear Alain. You have been so kind, it is hard for me to tell you directly how glad I am to know you, so I'll try to explain it in writing. Good feelings between people can take many forms. Please understand that I will be quite content if we can remain friends, and I look forward to our continuing friendship. Thank you for everything. I hope you will accept my sincerest best wishes.* I posted this in Rita's mail slot. The following day, in my own mail, I found a small chocolate bar called Yes, and a tiny bottle of lily-scented oil. Her note, in that deliberate, round hand, said *merci mille fois.* A thousand thanks.

As the semester neared its close, the weather never got any better. Every day I cranked open the wooden-slatted awning—to find the same lead sky and freezing rain. I had become immersed in the usual last-minute crises of my students, with final exams, faculty convenings—all the detritus that teachers mock and at the same time, to which they devote themselves with a kind of annoyed urgency; organizing their lives to attend and fulfill.

Amid those weeks I often walked a few blocks after dinner, allowing the cold to clear my head for the evening's stack of reading; one night as I rounded the corner at St. Jacques and rue de la Santé, I saw Rita through the brasserie window. She was sitting alone with a glass of red wine, a small brown ceramic carafe beside that, and—to my astonishment—a cigarette in one dangling hand. She looked at no one. She did not look well. I dreaded contact with her and, despising myself, hurried past the window. At about 11:30 that night I was wakened by the old-fashioned shriek of the dorm telephone.

"I need your opinion," she said.

"Can it wait until morning?" I wondered.

"Please."

I dressed, and went downstairs to find Rita waiting in the lobby. She wore a rumpled fuchsia sweat suit; her hair was a bit matted on one side. She smiled briefly, but her eyes seemed wild.

"Let's walk," I said. We pushed open the big glass doors and stepped into the dark chill. It still smelled of rush-hour exhaust. Students were hanging from the waist out the dorm windows above us, splashing beer, waving and hooting at each other. We walked toward Alésia, the middle-class neighborhoods lined with apartment buildings, many of their lights still on, though it was a Sunday night and they would be herding their toddlers to school in a matter of hours. Rita did not glance up at the apartment windows as I did, but studied their dull reflection in the damp pavement as she walked, and spoke.

Rita and Alain had had another date at Vincennes, during which they had ridden in a little mock train car around the Parc Floral, eaten ice creams, and had several photos of themselves snapped by someone with a Polaroid; Rita clutched the pictures like pressed flowers as they walked along the cold banks of the manmade pond. Alain had told Rita he cared deeply for her and wanted no harm to come to her, and Rita had finally been unable to contain her yearning: she had asked Alain why she could not come visit him or call him where he lived. Alain had again blamed his bizarre conductor schedule, and the fact that the loaned apartment had no phone. *C'est pas la peine,* he assured her. Don't worry about it. It's too much hassle. He put his arms around her and kissed her. He would call her.

Three weeks passed, and Rita decided, toward the end of that time, to get her French tutor's help looking for Alain's name on Minitel, the French computer Internet directory. Rita told her tutor she was trying to locate an old friend. After some effort poring through the columns on the printout, the two women found "A. Lemieux" among the Reims listings. It was the only one in Reims.

We were passing the black glass of the patisserie windows, toward the Parc Montsouris and the university. Occasionally an indistinct figure would approach and silently pass, yanked along by a sniffing dog on its leash.

"What did you do?" I prompted her after a moment.

"I phoned the listed number," she said simply.

"And?"—disgusted with my own eagerness.

"A young woman's voice," Rita said after a moment.

How young?

Girlfriend young. Wife young. And Rita's drawl was slow and entirely astonished, the way it had been when she had told me about stepping onto the wrong train. As if trying to state the case in a way that made sense, like an equation. Call a number, hear a woman.

The third secret, I thought.

And then? I urged her on. I wanted to hear the sound of the

man frying like an electrocuted bug. I felt a sort of furtive, angry glee, like someone who could not stop licking stale icing from a cake.

Rita had hung up. Then she had gathered the Polaroid snapshots of herself and Alain at the park, and written an intimate note as best she could, in French. *Chèr Alain, remember these, I hope they please you, until next time, with all my love.* She had carefully wrapped the note around the Polaroids and mailed them to the address given for A. Lemieux in the Minitel listings for Reims.

I said nothing for a minute. Then I said, "Let's head back."

I glanced at her as we walked, but Rita never looked up from studying the sidewalk. I could see my breath, and hers. The cold was seeping through my thin leather soles; my toes were numbing. We didn't speak again until we reached the dorm and sat in the empty, fluorescent lobby, perched on the edge of the abstract metallic seats by the big coffee table, like a couple of talk-show types. I asked her to tell me the rest.

She looked at her lap, at her clasped hands. Two days later, Rita told me, Alain called. She had asked him whether he had yet received something in the mail.

His voice had grown stiff, and wary. No. Why, he had asked.

Rita told him the Minitel story.

Alain, she said, had become frantic on the phone. *"C'été pas moi, Rita! C'été pas moi! C'est pas juste; tu n'as pas le droit!"* It wasn't me! It's not fair! You've no right! And he had hung up on her.

Rita looked at me in mild wonder, like a child waiting to be told about the moon's pull upon the tides.

"Yes," I suddenly said. "Yes. It was exactly what you should have done. The son of a bitch conniving bastard." My own language startled me yet did not supply the punch I craved.

She smiled wanly. "I'll go to bed now," she said.

I took her hands.

"Rita. Semester's almost finished," I said. "You'll be fine. You'll be out of here soon."

I watched her walk to the elevator and give a little nod before she entered.

I didn't hear from Rita thereafter, or see her again, until the last day of the program.

The cold had, in final days, given way to muggy heat, though the sky was still the color of silt. I was packed and waiting in the lobby, with my luggage, for the taxi to Charles de Gaulle. Though it wasn't a full-fledged graduation, it had all the queer earmarks—an odd and giddying weightlessness, the sense of roles and hierarchies erasing, of imminent free fall. A bus for the students was already rumbling outside; they were stopping in excited little huddles to exchange addresses and embrace and swear to keep in close touch. The young women were triumphant, perfumed and rouged for the plane flight, during which they planned, they said, to take over the aircraft for "a big trans-Atlantic party." Some of them had found their temporary French boyfriends; those less certain had pretended to; the shyest and plainest had taken refuge in furious all-night group journal-writing sessions, or in going to pray at Sacre Coeur.

Beyond the milling students I saw Rita slip through the dorm's glass doors. She was carefully groomed, in black sweater, slacks, and a brown suede jacket. Her blue eyes bulged under fresh makeup, carefully applied. Her hair had just been brushed out from the hot-curler set. I stood to signal her. "Here!" She raised her eyebrows, and walked to me in that carefully placed gait— what was it like?—like someone practicing to walk, balancing a book on her head for finishing school. Practicing in the waiting room of the life she hoped to lead.

I sat her down. The noise from the crowd of students was ricocheting through the big room; I had to yell to ask Rita her plans. Rita was not leaving Paris, it seemed. She had heard again from Alain. He had phoned.

I gaped at her. "What are you saying. What are you telling me?"

Rita smiled, a mysterious twitching at the corners of her mouth. She said Alain told her he wanted to see her once more. She had decided already, she said, to try to stay in Paris anyway, try to find a job in the champagne country, and now, also, so she could see him. But first she would look for an apartment here in Paris, she said, to figure things out. She had just a little money left, and she thought she would try to set something up here with it. What did I think? She searched my face. Did I think that was all right?

"Rita." I looked at her, and had to boom my voice to make myself heard above the shrilling kids. "If you have any money left at all, you need it to get a foothold back home."

"It might be something completely reasonable, something I can understand," she yelled back, and she colored, and the corners of her mouth twitched. I realized she was talking past me, about Alain's chicanery. And then I grasped it: *Soyons raisonnable. Tu peux me comprendre.* She was quoting his words. Rita had skipped a chapter in today's report. She had already met with Alain since his call; he had persuaded her of some shabby nonsense; she had slept with him. Because anything was better than waiting in the waiting room. Anything, anything at all, was better than that. I saw my taxi pull up in front of the dorm, and I rose to slice my way through the screaming twenty-year-olds. I took a step back from her, turning to flag the cab driver. Rita's hand went to my arm. "It might be just the right direction . . . I can keep up my French," she was shouting. "Don't you agree, Emily? Don't you think?" And blanketed by the din, her voice trailed off, in familiar, imploring, quavering, watery hope.

The Extraordinary Member
of Carlos Artiga

People who do not know him treat Carlos as if he were like any man.

He is not like any man.

Carlos Artiga is not tall, but he has a peculiar massiveness, a great solidity. His presence in the room is like the thickened trunk of a fantastic tree. His limbs are dense, bulging; they can crush. He wears his clothing loosely, but the contours surge heavily against the cloth. His skin is rough, like tree bark. His body has endured every manner of physical ordeal and in exotic response has grown a sort of inuring tissue, head to toe. Yet his hands remain quite small, creamy and smooth as a child's, as do his feet. His face too is smooth, neither young nor old, peering like an ageless bird's.

Carlos Artiga projects a tremendous force, or force field. The only proper way to convey the mightiness, the druggy viscosity of it, is to compare it with a cane fire. If you have lived where sugar cane is burned you know the pulsing heat and crack of it, rippling and popping with flying cinders and dense sulfurous smoke, heat and choking thickness rising and welling at some distance from the actual blaze. The closer you come, the more you risk.

Carlos was born in a tropical place where Spanish is spoken, and where the sex of the people swings freely and joyously as the clappers in bells. Where Carlos was born, the air is heavy with scents of waxy raw blossoms and frying meat and sticky liquors of ripening fruit. He was bathed in the salt sea and fed sugary cakes, and later he drank rum, and, surrounded by the perfume and talcumy sweat and lilac hair oil of his *tios* and aunties and cousins, his body's memory swelled with this blast of color and smell. He was a mild and sweet child who came as a young man to my country, and while he has made many friends and had vivid adventures here, beneath his skin, circulating through flesh and organs and sometimes filling his eyes like effervescent juices, he carries the sad and beautiful memories of his infancy in the old land.

Carlos Artiga was bequeathed an unexpected legacy. (No one can pinpoint how it happened. His father and brothers are reasonably physical men, satisfied with themselves in these realms, appreciated by their women, but none extravagantly so.) Between his legs dwells a phenomenon that many will likely never see—perhaps even if they saw, they would not believe; certainly *I* will likely never again view such in this life.

It is magnificent even when it sleeps.

Even then, it makes itself felt. It presses and shifts against his trousers like a lazy dog, kicking in its dreams. One cannot help letting one's eyes drift there, to begin to apprehend and measure its agreeable nature. The creature lifts its head joyfully, stirred by as much as a glance, shamelessly craving the slightest attention. Never did you know such vitality as to feel, even accidentally, the sudden wakefulness of Carlos's member, the bounding, begging, insistent pushing and prodding. It seems to be the engine of a larger being, the conductor of a reverberant power, as the engine room of a great ocean liner might hum and palpate.

His member tells Carlos the time. It wakes him, makes him doze, leads him from room to room, demanding its bath and airing. It is his barometer, his metronome, his tutor. If he is ill, it informs him so and instructs him in methods of care. The size of it—ah. Let us say that the fisted forearm of a large man might not compare in dimension to the fully wakened member of Carlos Artiga. Truly, it is an unnamed wonder of the world, and poor Carlos its shy and weary chaperon. For it troubles him no end, and he sighs frequently with the weight of it.

When it commands release Carlos has no choice. He will not be able to undertake the day's appointments until the tyrannical member is given its way. And that is when I am often pressed to duty, and I cannot pretend to you that this is a duty I am always pleased to perform. My work is arduous, uncomfortable, requiring great endurance and tricks of breathing. There has only been a bit of blood, but I would be lying to deny that I have suffered. Still, I rush to help him, to do what is needed like a triage nurse, because I have no heart to refuse poor Carlos, seeing how it sorrows him, the burden of serving this voracious master; it is a curse on him, unceasing, a separate function in a separate room that must be attended before he might ever turn to the calmer duties of this world. It exhausts him and makes him lonely.

Who can help Carlos? Who can truly comprehend it? Who else is so imprisoned in his own life, indentured forever to his own insatiable part? Were it up to Carlos, he'd surely prefer to lie floating in a rowboat on a hidden pond with his straw hat over his eyes, dozing, listening to the *whip-porbula-wheep-weep-weep* of a bird call, or to press the jewel pastes of watercolors on porous white paper, rendering a purple-yellow iris in the afternoon light—or to sit beside the open window practicing an ancient air on his wooden lute. The leisurely peace of these pastimes must seem to Carlos luxurious beyond saying, for the extraordinary member of Carlos Artiga is subject to no one. It is lord.

I am fortunate that I need see my suffering friend only twice a year, when business brings him to my city. But each visit looms for me, a grave ordeal. I must prepare well. I must take adequate rest, and exercise and nourishment, allow only the most serene thought. I must clean and cook and drape myself in beautiful vestments, so as to achieve an axis of calm, a plumb line of clarity. I will need all my power to help poor Carlos.

He will arrive at the airport with his customary nervous sweetness, rumpled overcoat draping that tree-trunk torso. I am always touched to see this dear man, shy, pleased, dense as an oak door, walking toward me with the tender, deliberate, careless bravura of any of the thousands of others around us on a city day. It makes me ache and love him more to recall his burden: he is not like the others. We will embrace fondly, Carlos and I, glad friends reunited, and we will drive somewhere to drink and talk and compare our lives, and at first the time will pass agreeably.

But soon enough the talk will falter and sputter as his member begins to knock restlessly between us, hammering—first at him, then at me, knocking and yanking like an overlarge, jealous child growing crosser and crosser. Finally there is no further hope for talk: exchanging doleful glances, sighing wearily, beleaguered parents to the furious junior, we'll have to rise and make our way to the hotel.

The Queen of Worldly Graces

You best remember Cal standing at your opened front door on a February Sunday in the pouring rain. An old borrowed car packed with Cal's things idled in the driveway, wisps of white exhaust floating into the raining afternoon, motor glub-glubbing. Cal wore a new raincoat over jeans and a long-sleeved madras shirt, and he was panting from having leapt up the front stairs. (Cal leapt everywhere, always breathless.) He wore a hat that morning, which, with the raincoat, made him look like an extra from a Ray Milland movie. "Jenny. Jenny. How are you, dear." Cal had a way of saying things several times, as if he were formalizing them for himself and for you; at the same time you knew he was buying time for his own thoughts to rocket ahead, ricocheting between a riotous splay of possibilities. Could he store his few things under your house? He was on his way to Paris the next day.

Your heart sank. All you'd wanted that Sunday was to brood over the *Times* in rainy peace. Tom was at a football game in the city (you'd forced the umbrella on him); Cal had not been expected until evening. But you smiled brightly and wrapped a warm lilt around your voice. These episodes have a resonance you know you'll be revisiting—yet how often you've wished you could simply skip the present tedious theater of it. You wish for more time in your pink plaid flannel robe. "Of course," you crooned. "Come 'round the back."

Cal believes himself a brilliant social scientist, convinced he will become beloved for his gifts, revered with age like a Bertrand Russell or a Gregory Bateson. He sends his tracts and treatises— presumably about human will and moral behavior, incompre-

hensible to you—to European universities, which he swears receive him far more intelligently than anywhere in America. In
Bonn and Lille they've invited him to lecture, but in Sacramento he's only invited onto cable TV talk shows that air at 4 in the
morning. The rest of his time Cal argues with colleagues about
fate and destiny: spirited beery debates in the sticky dark bars on
the old side of town—bars near the community college where
he teaches part-time, because Cal has no car and the bus system
is spotty. He argues at such a pitch that it puts half his audience
in a permanent fuddle. *He seems to be onto something,* they think
as they watch him waving his arms and thumping one balled fist
repeatedly into an open hand.

Calvin Grant is forty years old, son of a conservative Texas
judge, younger of two brothers. (His elder brother is gay, a pianist in a tony Dallas club at the top of a skyscraper.) The brothers are estranged from their parents, who live in a more or less
permanent sense of betrayal by their sons. Both sons have
shunned the family money, attached as it is to dourest condi-
tions.

Cal has medium-length, slightly kinky hair parted in the middle like that of a court page in a medieval painting. He is not a
handsome man, but his urgency lights and propels him like one
of those kiddie cars you stroke against the floor and release to
watch zip into a wall and flip over, sparks popping from its little
wheels, still revving. Cal's body is shaped in the pleasant invert-
ed triangle of a manly form. Yet his face, while no particular fea-
ture of it is outright bad, lacks that single odd or dear aspect that
might bring it forward in women's imaginations.

But it had not mattered about women's imaginations when
you first met Cal, because he had for many years been claimed
and adored by a patient young woman named Gina. They had
known one another since both were undergrads at the state college, and for nearly that long had lived in the top floor of a de-
crepit Victorian in old-town Sacramento. Though stifling in
summer and freezing without insulation in winter, and though
junkies and grifters stumbled past at all hours, leaving currents

of bad smells amid the jasmine, it suited them. The old trees were lovely, canopied motheringly over the streets. And the rent was low. Cal could play his Mahler loudly, the neighbors below either away or stoned insensible. Here he would air-conduct his favorite passages sitting cross-legged at his old word processor, or pacing before one of the large bay windows with the glass that seemed to ripple. Cal and Gina had lived many years in three rooms on the third floor, opposite a condemned storefront, and never bothered with curtains: at night the streetlight and the moon combined to pour raw cool white over the floor, over the mattress, the books, changing it all to white marble or lava, a temporary Roman frieze.

Tom knew Cal and Gina from undergrad classes at State; he had liked them both. When Tom moved to the little town on the north coast where he'd accepted a job, he'd invited Cal to visit.

"They're nice," Tom had shrugged when you pressed him for particulars the night before you were to meet them. "I've known them forever." You'd only known Tom then about a year, determined like all new lovers to learn his life and impress his friends. Amazing, how little men would reveal when you asked for background, for any debriefing. Perhaps men were embarrassed by how little they themselves knew; how little they sought to know.

"Well, what is it about Cal that keeps you interested?" you finally asked as you set the table. The evening sun was sending last pewter rays at a low slant through the kitchen windows.

Tom, tossing salad, arced his thick brows and widened his eyes: his "search me" expression.

"He's a bit crazy; bright, ambitious."

"But are you dazzled by his thinking? Do you expect great things of his work?"

A pause. "I'm never sure I completely understand it," Tom said to the salad bowl.

Gina was a translator, finishing doctoral work in French literature. She was thin, dark haired, with the black liquid eyes such types seem bound to own. She spoke with gentle wit, giving the sense she was old enough to have seen some things and not too old to have given up on others. As you passed the Caesar salad and the red wine, watching and listening to her, you found you liked her. She wasn't going to be hostile or neurotic, or to preen or pout. The four of you spoke that night with animation that soon relaxed into amity, Cal presiding with that great boyish zeal of his. At any moment it seemed he might jump onto the table or stick his head out the kitchen window and howl with pleasure, with the urgency of his quest—and his quest was perpetual, voracious. At first this seemed charming, but over time Cal's displays had come to make you feel lackluster and annoyed—his volubility took over a room. He seemed to be forcing some sort of contest, leaning forward with that hectic light in his eyes, the light of street-corner zealots. Whether or not Cal staged his antics consciously, you were aware of his pumping the stakes of a situation, aware of his careening mind, his rapid calculations and dismissals—he lent proceedings a sudden largeness that would burn into memory and echo later: *those days at Tom and Jen's when we were all struggling and eating cheap dinners.* You noticed, during these sessions, that Gina watched Cal with a kind of practiced patience, her face a studied neutrality you could not place, neither exactly fond nor cold. You noticed too that Cal rarely turned to confer with her, to glance or murmur some private reminder as couples will; instead he concentrated on directing himself in performance.

Both Cal and Gina—when she could get a word in—did ask after your own life, your magazine job in the city, your bad commute, your brother in Tucson, your bicycle tours. Neither seemed too handsome or too crazy, you decided. Neither would present Tom with a more attractive option. (This reflex shamed you; though you disliked it all your life on the faces of other wives and girlfriends, there it was.) You noticed with relief that Gina dressed like any ordinary student: jeans and a soft, nondescript shirt. Her hair was short, her face clean of makeup. You could feel generous toward this eccentric couple. You could even fancy affection for them.

And yet you had felt the tiniest fillip of anxiety about them in your breast as you washed the dishes that evening, couldn't find the slippery seed of it except to know it had to do with Gina, with a hooding glitter in her eyes. Her contained listening.

"They're lovely," you'd said to Tom after that first dinner, as he gathered plates and residue in quick, expert scoops. You said it unhappily, accusingly. Tom heard it.

"Of course they are; I told you they were," he said. He stopped to gaze at you. His voice carried roused attention: waiting for you to let out more line, which he would gently tug. Tom was alert to cues; he was good for your grimness, and you loved this un-ruffled patience of his. It was one of the reasons you'd left the city to move in with him. They didn't grow gentle, faithful men on trees.

"It's just—what," you left off lamely, looking deep into the thousands of opalescent dish suds as if they might form a holo-gram to explain it for you. "Something is—pained about it. Off-balance."

"Well, Cal is completely mad; that might affect matters," he offered, depositing another pile of soiled saucers at your elbow.

"Yet they've known each other so long," you murmured, more to yourself than Tom. You soaped and rinsed and stacked. Your hallowed thinking spot, the sink, the rainbowed bubbles, sel-dom seemed to make you smarter.

"And life is full of surprises," said your longtime lover, cock-ing his head, smiling. "Who knows what's really going on over there?"

"I want them to stay happy together," you said, turning to face him as if he had it to grant. As if you were a toddler requesting the corner piece of cake, the one with the most icing.

"Of course you do," he said, kindly. And he moved to take your face between his hands, as if to draw off its unease.

When next did you see Cal, before he wound up at your door in the rain? Let's see. There were the visits he made to Tom, when they walked the beach and hashed the most grandiose ideas about truth and reason and artistic morality. (Tom curated the small museum whose dedication ceremonies, five years ago, had brought you from the city to cover the event for *City Arts.* Discreet mutual measures were taken, phone numbers exchanged, Italian dinners eaten, bed with candlelight.) But you weren't around during Cal's beach walks with Tom; you were at work—the men had flexible schedules, you had nine to five. And in those just-starting-out days you'd been pleased to think of Tom being entertained in ways that need not worry you. Then there was the weekend one of them, Cal or Gina, had a birthday—you cannot remember which, for in your mind then the two had already assumed that interchangeable status of a fixed item, when both names are uttered together in one breath. They'd invited their few friends and unlocked their street-level steel gate (just a hair ajar so that those who knew a party was upstairs could slip in) and given a barbecue in their third-floor flat. On the tiny back balcony they'd set up a hibachi, where they were grilling—it had touched you to see—a few sad hot dogs, a tofu burger. They couldn't afford more.

Since then, news had trickled back to you. Cal had gone to Paris a year ago (without Gina, because of expense, of course) as part of the semester abroad program. There he had met a woman. But you could not get much of a description from Tom about it, perhaps because Tom felt in some ways self-conscious about the episode; after all, Cal had confided in him. Her name was Claire. Daughter of an old French family which kept the honored tradition, a Paris apartment and a house in the country. Claire was beautiful and imperious—but this you did not know until Cal produced her photograph after dinner.

It seems to you now that Claire was actually a distant friend of Gina's family. She must have come to one of Cal's lectures—she had decent English; Cal had almost no French. Claire was very sure of herself, brought Cal to meet her mother and sister. They had their photos taken dining together in a posh *boîte*—the snaps you saw. She had money, and so could ease their passage through a maze of coffees and meals and sightseeing. Cal began to decide he had profound feelings for Claire. You can imagine how his reasoning leapt along. He tormented himself about the decision, came back to Sacramento and broke the news to Gina.

They continued to live together for a time after his announcement, according to Tom.

My God, you had said.

Part of the mystery was that Cal struck you as oddly nonsexual. You'd never felt the subtle air about him that indicated a man's sexual awareness, though in truth you had not felt the distinct lack of it either. Tom may or may not have known what kind of sex Cal had with Claire, but he'd never spoken of it. You knew Tom would be deeply curious to know, but men sometimes kept an unexpected coyness about such matters, and you could not shame yourself to ask.

How they must have suffered—you fretted to Tom—when Cal told Gina his news! They had been together so many years. Tom shrugged, but you could envision it: Cal straining for the words, whipping himself to finish a truthful description of the sequence. Say Claire had drinks with him after a lecture. Say she brought him to see her apartment. Say he stayed for more drinks or coffee. Say she expressed vehement admiration for his work; say she insisted she understood his intention. Say she told him—pacing, smoking, locking eyes with him—that she wanted to follow that intention.

You can see Cal handing it over to Gina like something shoplifted, his belief that he loved this exotic Other, the incredible fact that he would have to leave Gina. Then Gina's face. Gina's face! A mask over the internal siege; the world in which she'd dwelt crushed like a hastily stubbed-out cigarette. Her eyes so glossy and sad, a tender horse's eyes. What had Gina said to Cal? You imagined her upright, scarcely breathing, someone informed of a death, her eyes two night skies never leaving his face. Listening. Questioning him softly; drawing closed (with each of his replies) a wrap around her heart like a shawl. *Then this is what you must do,* Gina answers him (in your mind). She cannot own him. She will honor his choices. She loves him but bids him choose. Wishes him to choose.

Perhaps Gina told Cal that everything between them would now be changed forever, that it was not something she could help. Cal would have to accept this, because he was its instigator. No one has told you what Cal was thinking, but you have an idea.

Cal Grant was forty years old, broke, teaching part-time in a community college, and he had met a stunning Parisian woman who said, *Come live with me; we will be a team; I will help you get lectures, I will translate for you, I will introduce you to people who can help your career.* How she would do this, whom she knew, was unclear. But Claire was dazzling. Her figure was mannequin-perfect, her clothes the smartest, her almond eyes made up to stop anyone cold. She chain-smoked, always in the act of fishing for the pack and extracting one and lighting it and gesturing with it and repositioning the ashtray—it hypnotized Cal; even made him a little jealous of the intimate cracked red prints on the white paper. He told himself he'd come to care for Claire; their chatter had seemed to rush headlong on the momentum of their frosty breath that winter, in and out of brasseries and theaters, along the severe gravel paths in the Luxembourg. He knew she regarded him as a novelty, a kind of reverse-*chic* trophy, but it was a status nonetheless. If he closed his eyes he thought he could envision a life between them. He thought of Wagner, Picasso, Camus. All attended by adoring, beautiful women, as utterly, willingly subjugated as Friday to Crusoe.

Then Cal had to think of losing his poppet (as he called her): his waif, Gina. The calm, sisterly goodness of her. The shorthand they spoke after so much time; the cookie-dough smell of her, slenderness of her wrists and ankles—her languorous tenderness in lovemaking, the way she looked into an invisible hearth as she formed her thoughts. His reflex of telling her everything and the relief that always poured into him once he did. The *con-*

solation of her troubled him 'round the clock: the idea of separating her from his awareness seemed as violent as amputation, yet the process already seemed loosed and rolling; he felt like one of those silent film characters with one leg planted on each of two fast-separating ice floes. Gina had never complained in their years together; only watched him quietly. And while her glittering eyes might question him, her goodness had always somehow accounted for them both, lent weight and constancy to them, a couple's universe that she did the work of sustaining —without her, Cal sometimes thought, he would likely be an itinerant crank who lived out of cans, the sort whose smell followed him in public. He felt he was effectively carrying out her murder. Cal imagined himself—briefly, guiltily savoring the comparison—a modern Prometheus, his precociousness singled out for torture by the gods.

Several fervent phone calls to Tom later, it was decided. Cal would quit his job, cash out his tiny retirement fund, sell or store his few things, and fly to Claire in Paris. He would arrange work and visas with Claire's help, after arrival. Tom hung up the phone to tell you when he got Cal's news.

You felt struck as if by a hand. He really would go through with it. "But why? Who is this person? What does he know about her? And he's going to live in her apartment, her country, and he speaks no French?"

Tom lifted his opened hands, eyes wide, brows high—he was getting good at these gestures of large, elaborate distancing. Normally you loved his Abe Lincoln looks, his quick dark eyes. But not this face, which seemed to be working to present a steady blankness.

"But where is the fairness of it?" you demanded. "All Gina has done is be faithful to him and love him for seventeen years. And here is her reward? We're all supposed to shrug like good Californians and say *Whatever, man?* This is the way the story goes?"

You were at the kitchen table, having pushed away the article you were editing, a diet advisory for women, whose author, a

manic macrobiotic doctor, had insisted on no softening of his
hard rules. Tom pulled up a chair across from you, sat down, set
a beer on the table. He said, "Jenny. Cal is forty years old. He has
no money; his work is not getting the attention he thinks it deserves. He probably sees this as a last long shot that might spring
him. I'm not—" he added quickly as he saw your mouth inhaling to interrupt—"I'm not saying this is right. I don't yet know
what to think."

You pushed your chair back and rose, the heat rushing in your
head.

"But what happens to the Ginas of this world? How many
fucking times do we have to watch this play out?" Tom looked
away and his nostrils flattened; you knew he hated hearing you
say *fuck*. But he knew it was true: you could count at least three
of his friends in the immediate neighborhood alone who'd
dumped their loyal, longstanding loves for a shinier later model. It was certainly old, old news but it was news that was supposed to happen to faraway people, people in Sunday newspaper surveys and smug best-sellers and bad nighttime soaps. You
have never been able to make any man admit to the cartoonlike
blatancy of it, the humping-dog balefulness of it, this never-
ending reflex to plug into the acolyte—someone who'll sigh
with thankfulness and tuck herself around him tighter when he
declares, "And *that's* the kind of guy I am."

The numbing tediousness of it! Whenever a celebrity gets
caught with his stewardess or stripper or his transvestite pickup
and hung in public cross fire, the tabloids pawing over fuzzy
zoom-lens photographs like last scraps of meat, you can only
think, *Yes. Hang the idiot. Keep him from spawning.*

"How am I supposed to endorse this?" you asked Tom in a
lower, clenched voice. "What is the role of the woman who likes
the woman the man is dumping? A Hallmark card? *Godspeed and
warm best wishes?*"

Tom looked at you, the sweating beer between both hands.

"Jen, take it easy. He's my friend; I can't disown him. We don't
know the details."

No, but you could imagine them all right, clearly as the veins and spines of the golding leaves drifting now in the yard, the scarlet and pink rose petals scattering that fall, the wild walnuts that crackled under the car in the driveway. You could imagine a gothic scene: tears, words, miserable dumb pauses during which two people stared at their feet, the walls, gummy coffee cups, objects they had seen without seeing for seventeen years as they each privately sounded out the word: *ending*.

And Tom had invited Cal to dinner, to store his stuff under your house, and for the how-many-eth time you would have to be gracious to another goddamned betrayer.

And yet that rainy Sunday morning you'd smiled and chatted as you ushered Cal in through the side gate, and in your bathrobe helped him haul his boxes and his ten-year-old stereo under the house, piling them neatly on some old wooden crates; waving as he drove off. He had come back to have dinner when Tom returned from the game, and the two men had stayed up late talking. That evening was when Cal had produced Claire's picture. Her store-window mannequin looks had puzzled you, for they seemed a non sequitur to everything you'd understood about Cal's bohemian ways. He never mentioned Gina except to tell Tom, late that night, it had been "a nightmare."

Next morning he was gone.

A note came in the mail six months later.

The thing had crashed.

Crashed like one of those terrifying visions at an aerial show, the sputtering plane bleeding black smoke as it spirals nose-first, straight down. The message scribbled in harsh black pencil lead, in what appeared great haste, pressed down hard.

It did not work with Claire. I tried but it went all wrong. I am teaching again in Sac and working in a map store. If you want, leave a message at the social sciences department. It went very badly. I did not contact you sooner because it is hard for me to talk about.

Tom phoned the school several times and left messages, dropped a note into the mail, but no answer came. It threw him in ways you could not have anticipated. One morning after he'd sifted through the mail—usual ads and bills—he walked through the house adjusting the paintings where they hung, a compulsion you'd always found maddening and dear. Nothing in the mail, and he had waited months for any word from Cal. You came from the kitchen in time to watch him walk to the sunny front window; turn around, sit down on the couch, get up and walk again to the window, hands fisted in his pockets. He looked at the quiet street, wide, clean, the leaves turning. You looked too. Through the window you saw a squirrel pause on a phone wire, sniffing, plume tail floating.

"No news from Cal yet, huh?" You felt badly for him in spite of yourself.

"The thing is." Tom spoke without turning around, in a voice you did not quite recognize, as if it came from some other room in him. "Some stories, you want to see how they work out, because you always wanted to know if they *could*." He was not looking at you. He seemed to be having an argument with himself. "I mean, if a man is forty and gives up everything to go try a dream life, to start again, it's different than when he's twenty or even thirty."

"Go on," you said, leaning in the doorjamb with your arms folded.

Tom sat again at the edge of the couch, hunched slightly, forearms resting against his knees, posture of a man in a waiting room. He opened his big hands. "The risk is wilder, but so is the need," he said in the same unfamiliar voice. "Every man has Cal's idea," he said softly, glancing at you a scant moment. "Every man thinks about it."

"I see." Astonished he would let you glimpse this.

"But most men know better," he added swiftly. You knew this to be spin control, but the gesture pierced you.

"So this was an experiment you were observing."

"Sort of." His eyes tracing some middle distance.

Last week a message from Cal appeared at last on the answering machine. His voice was sprightly and bounding again. He was on his way to Paris again. Could he stop through?

Tom went to pick him up at the bus station. You wished you had anywhere else to be, but it would look too obvious to run off, and you could not restrain a horrible curiosity. Cal burst into the house with the same old urgency, as if he'd just parachuted in. Same kinky curls, dull clothes, same lack of anything dear in his face. He looked agitated. You moved to buss his cheek; he seemed to shrink away. Did he sense your dim view, or had Tom told him? Was he embarrassed? Repulsed? Tom had set up chairs on the front porch so the two could sit and smoke. You remembered errands and, saluting them, slipped away.

They were more relaxed when you pulled the car back into the driveway. Cal actually asked to see your editing office, a converted shed behind the carport. You invited him in with alacrity, told him to sit, made a fire in the blackened potbelly some prior tenant had installed. As you did Tom entered to deposit a bottle of wine, then left to start dinner. You stirred the fire, put on a tape of baroque guitar. Cal was eager to talk and himself brought the conversation to Paris.

Going back to the city, he insisted, was a way of testing the worth of his work on its own merits, without help. He would make the rounds. There were daily humdrum realities—and then there was Paris. The two zones were never interchangeable; Paris was a proving ground like no other. The cold, the indifference, the expense, the grime—all of a piece. You listened patiently and finally asked.

"Why are you going back to Claire, Cal? What is going on?"

His eyes immediately hooded and seemed to cast themselves out the window. "Closure, maybe," he said unsteadily, after a beat.

It was a latter-day term that tightened your jaw.

"But Claire was the one who sent you away before. She smashed your life to bits. What happened? What do you think will be different this time?" Earnest scientist in a lab coat, trying to keep the prosecuting edge from your voice.

"She became frightened by the permanence of it last time," he said quietly. "When she saw me with my bags, it overwhelmed her, she said. It was the *bags,*" he repeated, as if reminding himself of the pivotal error, the curse never to reinvoke, as if everything that had gone wrong since was the leering result of his fatal miscalculation: the decision to bring luggage. "But now she says she misses me. Says her life's not the same without me. I want to see what is there for me this time." His words made you wince, they sounded so stagy. "I'm staying in my own hotel room, at my own expense," he added with a kind of wounded indignation. Cal, petulant! He had carefully fashioned his stance. He meant to maintain an offended front, a defiance: she would to have to penetrate it to win him back.

It was difficult for you not to snort. His scholarship might be brilliant, you thought, but he understands even less of himself than you'd imagined. Or—perhaps more likely—he's lying to spare your feelings. But since when had Cal considered anyone's feelings but Cal's?

"And what of Gina?" You had to ask it; no sense pretending. He stood up at once, and as you knelt by the fire you made yourself look straight up at him.

His face had voided. He looked neither angry nor sad, but as if he had been asked to speak of someone who had been dead for some time. His voice was similarly flat. "She won't speak to me. She'll have nothing to do with me now."

Tom cracked open the door: dinner summoned. He had laid on a homey one, a roast with vegetables. You mashed the potatoes with annoyed energy, knowing you were enacting, for Cal to witness, Tom's answer to Cal's implicit question: *Yes, this life with her is good, and it is enough.* But you also knew this meal was Tom's gesture of solidarity with Cal, offering fortification, ballast. Something irritatingly biblical about it. *Take this for sustenance on your path, brother; hold fast to your journey.* Cal ate heartily, accepting seconds. The three of you watched a Hitchcock movie. Finally you begged off to bed because of work next morning, while the men stayed up for a last smoke. You slept hard, not noticing when Tom slipped under the covers. Next morning you showered and tiptoed in the dark out to the bus stop; that night when you walked back in, of course, Cal was gone.

"Well? What did he have to say?" Working to keep your voice breezy as you tossed your coat and bag. Technically you had no right to the information, but you would force the matter if necessary, and Tom knew it. At once his voice muted, his facial features blurred—he'd suddenly ceased to be the inhabitant of his own body.

"Something about beauty," Tom murmured.

"What? I beg your pardon?"

"Beauty. *Beauty*," said Tom again, too loudly the second time. "Cal has this idea about beauty." It seemed Gina, in Cal's eyes, had become an embarrassment. A holdover from flower-child days in free-box clothes. She was actually (Cal told Tom) more a boyish sister at this point, the one who'd looked after him. Gina had short-cropped hair and wore no makeup. Never bothered with her nails; wouldn't think twice about wearing jeans with a hole at the knee. (*Neither do I; neither would I*, you thought, cheeks hot. And what about Cal's own hodgepodge style? *Above such concerns*, presumably. *Eyes on the stars*.) Whereas Claire was a woman of the world. Coiffed, fragranced, perfectly finished and lacquered; clothes and manners de rigueur. Heads turned where she passed. Cal had decided that a man of his capabilities, of the regard he anticipated—and he fully anticipated that regard—now deserved that level of beauty on his arm. Claire was classic, pristine, a Grace Kelly or a Deneuve. Gina was an urchin, a street mime. Cal had felt a premonition. He was ready now, he sensed, to partner a stunning beauty; a level of grooming—*grooming* was the word Tom used—in the woman he takes, as part of his claim to his rightful destiny.

Tom murmured this in short sentences, prodded by your insistent, repeated questions. He could let his eyes meet yours only an instant before he'd flick them away.

You walked to the sink and leaned hard against it, arms around yourself tightly, looking out the kitchen window into the early dark. "Ah," you said. "Aha." The words batted about senselessly. "Right. Fair exchange," you said, nearly choked by the astonishment that had ballooned up in you, filling every cavity of you like some angioplasty gone haywire. "Of course. They deserve each other," you said with a lightness so forced it edged on hysterical.

"Jen, for Christ's sake." Tom was sullen. He hated the sound of his own voice conveying this howlingly bad script, the dripping egg of its punch line sliding down his cheeks. No way to shelter himself: he'd had to deliver it, and now you both had to say logical things to each other, continue to live together in the world, act as if you were sure of anything. Both of you caught like prisoners against the compound wall, pinned under the white-hot spotlight of the new reality.

You turned on him, your voice taut and cracking. "You feel this way in some part of you, and now you are watching to see how this chapter turns out."

"What do you mean?" Dully.

"Grooming. *Grooming* was always your obsession too," you said, your voice now thick inside an aching throat. Your eye sockets hurt. "When we were in Europe. You were ashamed of me. I did not match the local level of—of *gloss.*" The month you'd spent three years ago, a trip he'd taken for his institute: pricked with unhappy revelations that had almost finished off the two of you. Unmarried, you'd lacked official status trailing after him at functions. Perhaps what they say is true, that women remember all the worst moments: his telling you he needed space; telling you to go shopping with one of his comely colleagues, who had "instinctive style." The early evening you'd faced the Eiffel Tower together for the first time, leaning on a railing with your backs to the Trocadero, and you'd turned toward him, breathless, for a gesture. He'd only stared ahead at the Eiffel, mulling. You are certain now he was simply unconscious; he could have been adding up his bank balance. But it was your first trip together. Later he apologized and explained there was too much performance pressure on him: constant scrutiny by clients and colleagues. That you should simply forget that time, let it go. You'd felt he was struggling with a half-submerged wish to be free. Balancing it against an uneasy mix of guesswork and observation—about what, or who, was truly out there.

"I put all that away years ago," he said. He looked steadily at you, the way you might stare down a rattler at close range, not moving from his chair at the table.

"Nice try," you said. "Try again."

"I don't want to *be* him, Jen! I feel *sorry* for him!"

"Phase two of the Living Experiment: subject knighted by great beauty," you said bitterly.

"Jen, I want a house and vacations. I want to be warm and eat well. I want to have my best pal with me to laugh at my jokes. *I don't want to see the road through a hole in the car floor,*" he said. It was an old code-phrase between you, from a visit to an aging hippie friend who'd kept your own younger, shabbier ways—code for the scrappy, blurted life that was good for people at twenty and thirty but not so compelling (you'd both agreed) after forty. Tom came to you and took your shoulders, your cheeks. "Don't you see?" His voice cracked softly.

You nodded, exhausted. Why did it matter this much, anyway? Say you lost him to one type or another: wouldn't it be better to know that sooner than later? Why live in dread, anticipating a siege? It was just (you would answer) that summoning great gentility, smiling and nodding, accommodating foolish men like the queen of worldly graces was not what first came to mind when their women—lovely, complicated, credulous women—were recurringly toppled and swept from the board like faded toy soldiers. Where did they take themselves, these women? What happened next to them? And after that?

Get a life, people say. A life doesn't cringe. Too much cringing going on everywhere, to your thinking. You know one woman much older than yourself who insisted on walking the entire Bois de Boulogne in heels and hose, because she had long ago vowed never to be seen in anything less by her husband. You are sure she was temporarily crippled by the end of that day. You know another whose husband watches his wife get dressed every morning with an expectant air, waiting to be shown she can look good again. Make the grade again. Every morning.

A life stands in its own shoes. Says "This is what is, sweetheart. No character transplants or plastic surgery coming your way."

And it seems to you that as soon as you have said such words, whenever you tried them on like a shimmering green silk toga, a cool spaciousness filled you, a blessed lightness. Whenever you donned that thinking—when you thought *I'm too old to cringe,* in a kind of revelatory astonishment—then Tom seemed to feel the shift instantly, to seek you out. You think of the girlfriend who told you over drinks, shortly before she consented to marry—told you with sad, thoughtful finality, "Betrayal is not the worst thing, Jenny." Mystified, you had asked her what on earth the worst thing was. "Quitting the game," she sighed. "Disinvestment. Walking. Like Rhett Butler."

Tom was not quitting. Nor were you. But he would watch for the outcome of Cal's latest venture. Tom would always be watching for outcomes. Both of you would; no avoiding it—people's stories, including your own, would scroll out before you in the tides of all your coming days. And what would those outcomes teach you that was not already known—for which the evidence did not already lay piled about tall as mountains? You lay your cheek against him, put your nose into his warm neck with its cola-sweet man-smell, and clasped him hard. He tightened his embrace; both of you holding on like siblings against a high wind in a suddenly cold place. Though the sun that morning glowed through the windows clean and warm, you held on tightly against an icy wind that swirled and sang silently about you, trying to pry between.

The Scanner

He takes it with him everywhere.

On his days off he drives it to certain neighborhoods to get better reception. It looks like a little shortwave radio. You punch buttons and twist dials and listen in to people's cellular-phone conversations. Do this in a place like Oakland, and you are in for some drama.

He first learned about it at his job, maintaining the conveyors and mixers at the cookie factory in the heavy-industry section south of the city. It's another planet out there, cold and geometrical, and people only go there because they have to, to work. Landscape of a bad dream: all the buildings long and windowless and square, a series of giant hangars; air thick with exhaust, surfaces blackened. Sullen little bars with trembling, buzzing neon signs mark the street corners. He always smells like sugar and machine oil when he punches out. It's not the best work, but it pays okay. Sometimes guys lose a finger or hand in the belts. It's a code they yell over the intercom, and then everyone goes running to see who it was. He can't bring himself to look.

He has a wife whose voice is hard, and a mistress who finally said *Don't call me anymore.* He has a lot of time on his hands. He started listening to the scanner in the locker room, with the guys. They are like him, Latin and Asian, heavy from beer, living apart from daylight and clean clothes and Sunday brunches, strapped in for the long ride—in-laws and bills; no money and no prospects. They are fixated on pussy, their lockers papered with color shots, and on insulting each other in creative ways. Sometimes the insults go too far and a fight starts, but more often they're too tired to fight. They all tune in to the scanner at lunch, which is at midnight, and on breaks, at 3 and 5 A.M.

Once they clearly heard a call girl give a man her telephone number. They decided to phone the number to find out what she charged. It was two hundred. They were falling off the benches, they were laughing so hard. They couldn't get up the nerve to ask her what specialties she offered. But of course they guessed at a few to each other. Another time they heard the aftermath celebration of what may have been a murder. They heard some kids bragging that they were talking from someone's car phone, driving that person's car, saying that they were goofing with that person's gun. Then the kids fired the gun over the phone to prove it. Piecing together the words, the men imagined the kids had killed the owner of the car and taken the car, along with the victim's gun. He actually called the cops to report it, but hung up fast when they asked him who and where he was.

After a while he got tired of waiting for the one guy in the locker room to bring out his scanner. And he got tired of telling the others to shut up so he could hear better. Like a ham radio or a war walkie-talkie, the machine made a staticky background crackle, and you had to stay very quiet and strain your ears hard to make out the snippets of voices slipping through. The others' guffaws made him miss pieces of the voices. The missing pieces could have been important. He finally went to the electronics store and sprang two hundred bucks for one of his own. He figured he worked hard.

He was patient, twisting and adjusting the dials, searching the bands. Eventually he'd hear something.

Once he heard two cops talking about how someone in the projects had killed another cop—but there was no way to pin it on the guy, not enough cops to scare up some proof. "We'll just have to take him out ourselves," one cop then said thoughtfully to the other, over the scanner. *Take him out.* That really got him.

Another time he heard two doctors at the famous medical center, one younger and one older. The older one was urging the younger one to "meet with them. They are ready to meet with you." The younger one sounded agitated and scared. It had to do with running drugs, and it was organized from high up. He thought about going to the place where they said they would meet, but at the last minute changed his mind.

He also thought about going to the restaurant where he'd heard a man set up a date with a woman, to see what the faces looked like that belonged to the voices. Something would always bubble up, if you just gave the machine a little time. Men called their mistresses and whores all night on their car phones, and men called to check up on men, too. The whores called each other and told each other what their tricks had asked of them. The air was full of voices, the voices full of secrets. People were high and driving, or fixing, or packing money and weapons and hard-ons. Drug lords swore death to their rivals. In the badass neighborhoods he heard men call women in the small hours, 3 and 4 A.M., and tell them what they were going to do to them when they came over. He could hear the women's babies crying in the background. One time a woman said her baby was real sick and had to go to the hospital. The man calling her offered to drive her and the baby, but the woman said she was waiting for her baby's daddy to come get them. The man could come over and see her if he wanted, she said, but she was holding out for "my baby's daddy" to drive them to the hospital. This made his throat feel dry, but he never mentioned it to anyone.

When he listened to his scanner it was like stepping into an unlit room in which unspeakable things were taking place, moving sinuously, maddeningly. Turning the words over and over in his mind, he groped the hefts and shapes of those unspeakable things like a blind man, picturing the lights and darks and smells of them; the way the shapes moved and touched each other— hungering for the parts he could not see.

His mistress had got angrier and angrier because he would bring the scanner with him to her apartment and start fooling with it as soon as he sat down on the couch. He fiddled with it in the car while they drove somewhere to eat, and he would make her wait to get out of the car until he had heard out some conversation that sounded promising. She always felt a little sick when she saw him pull it out of its carrying case and start work-

ing the knobs, searching through the crackling static and patches of voices, his face tensed in an excited way. But what was
worse, even though she hated it, she started to want to listen, too.
This made her much angrier. You are looking up people's ass-
holes, she told him. You were made for better than that, she said.
He only looked at her, his face wide and sad as open hands. *And
what else have I,* his face seemed to wonder mildly.

Finally one afternoon she got out of the shower to join him
in bed. And he had the boxy black radio there in the bed with
him. He was pulling and pushing the antenna, twisting the
knobs, straining with all his features to hear through the wheeze
of static, to catch the snippets and ghosts of voices peeling off
like bubbles underwater, while he was waiting there for her in
bed.

That was it.

Now he drives around alone with the scanner in the passenger seat next to him, day and night. It sings to him mindlessly,
tunelessly, a blind chirping fountain of electronic babble like
those little robots in science fiction movies. He drives it to work
across the bridge in the moonlight, over water and under stars,
trolling the air for sound.

A Stalwart Girl

Myron had held his job a long time. It was a good job, as jobs go. Envied, really, by so many. To own a small, viable gallery in a choice section of downtown, walls hung with a few superb jewels to indicate the level of discourse Myron no less than demanded—to see the door open and the face filled with need insinuate itself into the crack of daylight, followed by the bulky corner of the portfolio itself—these realities always sent a frisson of pleasure through Myron, though he couldn't have said so. It was a power like few others. His word opened their lives to being noticed, to going on to awards and grants and possible fame, though in truth he could not claim to have shepherded anyone who was not already well en route—in fact, he tended to take them more readily when he had reason to be fairly sure of that. His arching brows (he was aware they lifted) as he gazed at their work samples, his carefully spaced, neutral acknowledgments (*mmm . . . yehhss*—a physician reviewing a specimen) kept his petitioners on tenterhooks. Often he asked to hold portfolios a month or two, further stretching the artists' anguish, causing them to tell themselves many stories about his likely response— and finally his brisk decline, penned in a spiky, hasty hand on a small white sheet of paper (fountain pen, medium nub, black ink)—always suggesting courteously that they try him again in future; he meant, they supposed, try him after having attained an ineffable level of mastery.

It was all to the good, this winnowing, Myron had long ago concluded. The fewer of these poor sons of bitches, the better. It was a game for the hardy, with talent and drive to spare, and those sort were precious few. The others would do well to learn bricklaying.

Myron would pass his days in the gallery reading, making phone calls, chatting up visitors, particularly those who ap-

peared to promise funding. If he sensed they were after one of
his basic jewels, the works he kept in the back room during
shows, he steered them toward another piece. The jewels had to
stay, as perennial bait. He scanned *ArtNews,* the auctions in the
Times, and the glossier journals for trends and patterns. He
lunched with the promising and with the monied—new and es-
tablished contacts who enjoyed his droll anecdotes—and year-
ly was able to replenish the overhead coffers for his gleaming
room. Myron went home promptly at five, carefully mixed a
shakerful of Bombay Sapphire martinis, watched one half-hour
of the *Lehrer Report* with his first drink and attended to dinner
with the second: generally a chop and a salad bathed in his own
dressing. Myron did not believe in bottled dressings. He did not
wear denim jeans. He hired people to clean his apartment and
dropped off his laundry. He did not take formal exercise but felt
walking did the trick and, anyway, was more seemly.

Myron also taught several university extension courses on
modern art and so had access to educational grants and resi-
dencies. He worked these like a professional broker: many
proposals filed at any given time yielded regular intervals of
foundation-funded travel all over the country, even to Europe.
This was especially important because although Myron's gallery
was nationally recognized, it was lodged (almost like a dropped
object) in a stunningly dull midwestern city. The city's very
name implied industrial grayness, Jell-O salads, backward baseball caps and pig-eyed stupidity—enervating in the extreme to
Myron, and much of the reason he traveled. Myron had two grown
children from a first marriage—one on each coast—whom he
rarely saw, and a second wife of possibly the best kind: a sales
director for corporate insurance, she traveled almost constantly.
They left each other voice mail. Life was orderly; sometimes, however, it seemed to Myron to rattle a bit for want of something—
or someone. Myron often stayed up watching television until the
screen went to white noise and all the martinis from the shaker,
with several more besides, were safely inside him. No one need-

ed to know, and except for the tiny red lacework of capillaries draping his nose, no one would.

Teresa Reed had been trying to get into the Pyramid Gallery for years. She had only begun offering her work, though she was not herself young when she'd sent the Pyramid owner her first set of slides—some abstract oils. And on the strength of these Myron Vandermeer had phoned and explained he had business in the Bay Area; could he have dinner with her? He found her paintings, a series of Mondrianish patchwork studies dense with color, appealing in some irrational way, a rawness of energy that seemed promising to him—or so he told Teresa. Teresa was then working as a receptionist for *Earth House Hold,* a Berkeley environmental newsletter. She drove a twelve-year-old Japanese hatchback with no radio, which she regarded as her escape-vehicle and protector. When she parked it at the restaurant where she was to meet Myron, she whispered a reassurance to the car as riders must to their horses. The restaurant she'd suggested was big and noisy, brimming with blue-collar workers swept in and out by loudspeaker announcement, affably drunk as they gnawed at bread and waited for huge bowls of fried things.

Teresa didn't know what to say to Myron Vandermeer, a respected name in the circuit. Was he serious about her work? She looked at him across the table—placid, somewhat florid. He was married, Teresa learned, with grown children, but though he answered her questions evenly, he seemed not to want to dwell on his own family. Instead he kept asking about herself, and she wondered at his stately formality—her uneasy sense was that it masked a faintly bemused irony; that he was interviewing an alien life form.

"And you say you have a sister in Wisconsin?" Eyebrows slightly floating.

"Well, yes, Racine. But I rarely see her. I can't often—afford it—" Teresa felt the warmth flood her face. She was sure Myron could afford a great deal. She was perhaps too old to be sounding this way, so beatnicky. But in fact she was paying off a master's degree, and though old enough to be driving kids to soccer practice, she lived alone in an aging apartment off the drearier end of Telegraph Avenue, indifferent to the cold little rooms in a way that horrified people. The rooms connected to a big, drafty studio, ample enough to roller-skate in. She loved the smell in there of her dented tubes of oils—like clay from deep in the earth, she'd always thought—smells of linseed oil and turpentiney white zinc. Loved her stained rags, lumps of charcoal, piled sketches, swatch of canvases propped against the walls. The smells of the room, the sight of its familiar components gave her back an ease of self, a deep exhale like the sigh that escapes in first moments of a hot bath. But this was hard to explain to peers who were taking out mortgages. A married girlfriend had emerged from Teresa's cramped 1930s bathroom with its rust-stained sink and announced, "I could never live this way again."

"Also," Teresa was telling Myron, "I hate eastern winters. It seems impossible to think, when your whole body is so contracted with the cold," she heard herself say.—Oh, dear. Another gaffe. Myron routinely endured nasty winters. He looked at her with what appeared to be a quickly stifled amusement, like the flicker of smile at the corners of Jeremy Brett's lips when he played Sherlock Holmes. (Teresa watched public television when she was too exhausted, after a full office day and then the hours at the easel, to stare at her canvases any longer. She would flop to the couch, put her feet high up on stacked pillows, and feel immediately the pleasant sleepiness when the blood in her legs was forced backward.)

"And you go to the smaller shows in San Francisco?" he prompted.

"Oh, yes," Teresa murmured. "I go to everything, as far as I trust the car to drive." She was taking up Cobb salad as efficiently as the fork in the right hand, and a hunk of positioning sourdough in the left, would allow. It was hard to chew decorously and still speak. "When the shows are good, they make me want to go home and paint for a straight week. They make me want to just not see anyone and go and go and go. I feel sad though sometimes," she added, looking away into air—"when I see the old masters. The lives they led; that they had to be such mad maniacs to get it done. And if they behaved horribly toward people who loved them, should I admire their beautiful work?" She looked back at Myron, and shrugged. "But then not much has really changed, has it?"

At Myron's silence, Teresa felt abashed again. She should shut up. He must think her an idiot, a dupe. Why else would he amuse himself this way? He had not offered another word about her paintings, only these sideways suggestions about trying other places, other people. Did he want sex? The problem flattered her an instant, then made her hugely tired. Teresa was not a special beauty, though she had lived with men and still got occasional looks from them. She was just attractive enough, she thought, to have had her share of adventures and to feel sorry for women at extremes of the scale—for raving beauties and exceptionally homely women alike. She disliked her nose, especially in three-way mirrors.

Myron's own roseate nose hadn't escaped her attention (she took care not to focus on it), nor his carefully deadpan expression (it must, she thought, be a cover for uttermost scorn). She was relieved when he announced another engagement and had to cut short the evening. Standing before him outside the restaurant door at the edge of the parking lot, relief made her almost fond. In his black overcoat, his expression appeared glazed. Teresa supposed he found the moment distasteful; that in fact he found most everything about her boorish, or—the word *jejune* floated across her internal vision like a bit of stray ticker tape. Teresa was not practiced at the manners of the reserved. She had given Myron some dinner money, and he had not refused it. Standing in the crisp cobalt air of early fall in Berkeley, she thought, *What's the polite thing?* and on impulse, shot a quick peck to his left cheek—it smelled of men's cologne. She thanked him cheerily and turned to stride to her old car. When she glanced back to see him still standing there, he started, and began busily to search his pockets.

She knew Myron Vandermeer had a plane to catch back to his city next morning. It was therefore mysterious to her when the phone rang at her office—"Earth House Hold, Teresa speaking,"—and Myron's voice, rather pinched and high, rose over the public-address noise of the airport, as if caught off guard in the middle of a distant country: "—Oh yes hello Teresa, it's Myron Vandermeer."

It was a confused and confusing salutation, one Teresa would hear for years. And for years she would never know what to do about it.

Myron would call Teresa at her office. He'd call her at home in the evening. He called her from New York, Chicago, Houston, Los Angeles. He called her from an airplane. He called her from hotel rooms, libraries, colleges. He called her when he was briskly sober, called her when he was caustically drunk, after far too many Bombay martinis with a tongue thick as peanut butter. (It was the only time he said a nice thing directly to her about her art: "You'rre a terriffich p-hainterr," he'd breathed late one evening into the phone. "Bless you," she had mumbled. She doubted he'd ever remember.)

Once in a while, saying goodbye at the end of a call, Myron's voice would grow a little husky. "Take care," he would murmur before replacing the receiver, and there would come at the end of that word *care* a helplessly tender croak, in which she clearly heard—briefly unhooded—an aching softness. A man she might, in some far parallel universe, want to know. It was the quickest opening and closing of a lens.

Soon she understood, however, that an arch *froideur* would rush back over this naked moment like the Ocean Beach fog—that he'd instantly again be hidden, seamless, sardonic as she breathlessly told him her news. If she made a sentimental mistake by appealing to him for any level of popular acknowledgment—"Oh, you know; you're a Dad!" she'd once urged gaily, to instantly regret it—the temperature dropped to freezing.

Myron knew he wanted an affair with the earnest woman who'd sent him work when they'd sat down to dinner that first night. He was perhaps ten years her elder—a pleasant, tenable distance—and if she was clumsy and rather a dilettante, she had such charming ingenuousness for a woman her age, with her black skirts and low heels and little navy blazers that fit so ripely; her comical urgency, her words a jangly goulash of high and low culture. But he didn't know how to tell her. For the first time since he could remember he felt shy, and his confusion annoyed him.

A thousand doubts. *She's not interested. She's unimpressed. Other men.* But then he would argue with himself: *I've encouraged her. I've made her laugh. We can both continue to have lives. She's a libertine, after all; she's seasoned. We could carry it off in a stately way. Phone calls, good dinners, hotels. Rendezvous when I lecture.* And he would rehearse the words of proposing to her that they go to bed.

He could never utter them. He phoned her but found himself speaking of anything else, so that they were forced to chatter energetically about gossip, weather, where his wife currently was—things neither of them gave a damn about. *Awkward*, he thought, miserably awkward. He flew home and drank martinis, rearranged his papers and stared at the television.

Her work had definite promise, but it was developmentally young; self-referential. And best, he thought, not to get entangled with it if they were to become lovers. It might compromise his own standards, and perhaps—far more dangerous—be discerned by others. It wasn't that such things did not happen, of course; look at Stieglitz and O'Keeffe—but the idea that his surgical impartiality might risk going soft and moldy—worse, that this might be noted—was unbearable. He congratulated himself on his rigor. There wasn't much of that left these days.

Myron sent Teresa cards from the museums he visited. The lovely Cézannes in the converted Maison Dubrujeaud, in Avignon. The little Giacomettis placed among indoor water gardens, in the seaside museum near Copenhagen. From Cambridge came a miniature of a twenties book cover, a Maxfield Parrish–style young woman in wind-floated gown poised like a brave heroine on the edge of a cliff, bonnet ribbons flying; its caption in old-fashioned typeface read "A Stalwart Girl."

Each time Myron phoned, Teresa would fish deeply in herself for a tone that sounded lyrical, though at the same time her heart would drop, dreading the strange minuet that would commence. She would ask after his health, his family, his work. He would tell her in his offhand way that he was acquiring someone quite promising for the Pyramid. Someone just given a show in the Village, someone just written up in the *New Yorker* briefs, someone just cited in a "best of" critics list. In fact he'd just taken several of that person's pieces, he'd add thoughtfully. *Really*, Teresa would chime like a society hostess. She spoke at first coolly, trying to mimic his airy nonchalance; later warmly, believing that ultimately he must actually offer warmth back; still later, fatigued, she grew reckless and spoke crossly, even angrily. She began to feel she was living in a satirical movie without end, the sort where everyone at the dining table turns into a rabbi.

Teresa had tried at first to applaud Myron's artistic finds, as if Myron's collecting the true talent were all that could possibly matter. Myron seemed to accede very happily to this interpretation: Teresa became an omniscient ear, as if there were no other reason for them to speak than that she marvel at his festive schedule, his acquisition triumphs. "Have a lovely summer in London," she would hear herself warbling mechanically from her reception desk, scrinching the receiver between shoulder and ear so her hands could unload boxes of file folders and sign for deliveries, wave *bye-bye* and *thanks* and *wait just a minute*. "Enjoy your Canadian tour," . . . your southern Cal tour, your Manhattan apartment.

Teresa knew before he finally told her that Myron wanted an

affair. And though she demurred *(think quickly!)* that she was already seeing someone, what she could never bring herself to say to him was *I do not know how to have sex with you; the idea is not manageable to me.* How could anyone say that to a man? Despite his silly loftiness or perhaps even because of it, her heart felt sore for him: remembering that sad, soft croak in his farewells.

Sometimes Teresa tried to envision becoming Myron's mistress. She would have to dress up and spray good cologne, and meet him for martinis and steaks. They would talk, get tipsy enough to feel unreasonably witty, go to a nearby hotel, and kiss. Teresa could see the Lysol-scented neutrality of the over-vacuumed room, its puffy-quilted bedspread, ships-at-sea print, chlorinated bathroom. She thought about sitting on the edge of the puffy bed kissing this man, tasting steak fat and gin. The unbuttoning of clothing, a certain quality of flaccid belly flesh, a descending intensification of hair. Faint, yeasty sweat. She thought of dirty socks peeled off, laying at skewed angles on the floor. And that was precisely when the projection machine snapped, flap-flapping, the film reel sputtering to a halt with a rude groan. *No,* said the projectionist, shaking her head with her eyes closed. *No, no, no.*

She hoped against hope that he might still take her paintings.

He took nothing.

She kept sending.

He kept phoning.

Myron Vandermeer scheduled his trips, taught his classes, and mounted his Pyramid shows to fine reviews, each a prudent balance of new talent with bankable names. In the late hours and at secret intervals, he called that woman out west, Teresa Reed. She only needed prodding—he was convinced of it, heard it in her voice when he telephoned, a battle of affection against caution. She could certainly have a boyfriend if she chose, as long as he, Myron, were spared the details—he never asked, and she never offered. But wry affection, yes: he was certain he could hear it, a tone of—pained warmth, it seemed, in her voice. She could be coaxed, if he persisted. If he occasionally suggested places she might apply for funding, that would show he was paying attention. She had asked for friendship. Friendship!—that miserable reduction, that pathetic euphemism. No, he'd keep trying. When Teresa's compassion had sounded most shapely, most womanly on the phone in those early days, he'd had a whiff of something they might almost slip into, like a silk kimono—but as quickly, the robe would slip off again. Myron sipped his drink as he clicked the remote.

After several years Teresa began to let go of pretenses. Her voice grew harder when Myron phoned, and she did not bother to hide her irritation at his airy greeting. She told Myron she was exhausted. She told him she was broke. Told him about the jobs she undertook when the ecology newsletter, losing funding, had laid her off—a temp secretary at the French consulate, the petroleum company, the congresswoman's headquarters. Told him how getting up at five to paint before work made her feel by the end of a week like she was being held underwater. Though from time to time a decent gallery would take a painting, and once she'd even managed to win a small out-of-state competition (three hundred dollars and her picture in the newspaper)—she was maddened by the lack of response to her efforts. Of fifty sets of slides sent (oh, the money it had cost!) two notes had arrived, one saying simply, *Good to see, Teresa.* Myron always went quiet at these outbursts. Then he would wonder, in a tone for inquiring after local weather—if there weren't more grants she mightn't apply for.

All this time, Teresa was sending Myron her slides. At first she took care to send him only paintings that seemed to fit with what she knew he'd first liked, rich abstract oils with bold use of color. Then she began to send him darker, more difficult pieces; attenuated, lopsided works. She sent a series of cigar-box paintings drained of all color except a formaldehyde-ish, corpse blue; charcoals that were raw blotches and cutting gashes. Antic collages of Greek sculpture body parts, fused onto obscene portraits of

Warner Brothers cartoon characters against pastoral hillsides. Miniature wooden sarcophagi with celebrity names scripted onto the lids in what looked like syrup, or blood. At last, she sent a potato.

A raw potato, with a form cover letter stating that the enclosed potato was herewith submitted for his review; if he were interested, she would be glad to make arrangements to show him more potatoes. She thanked him and enclosed a self-addressed mailer bag so he could return the potato if he were not interested.

He took nothing. He offered no comments. She was too wretched to press for any.

He kept phoning. Seattle. New Orleans. Saratoga Springs.

Once or twice, Myron sent a little note back with her slides. "Not quite finished"; or "Needs more certainty of brushwork"; or "Composition off somehow. Regards."

One Saturday Teresa stared at her drawers and began yanking out old files with the idea of destroying them, laying the oversized drawings on the floor like a game of giant solitaire. Out came a series of erotic pen-and-inks she had done when she was just beginning, the edges of the hard paper already going yellow and curly. Years ago she had trotted these to class, received a cryptic nod from the instructor ("I'm very impressed, Teresa")— shopped them around to galleries with no reaction, and sadly stuffed them away. She studied them now, wondering if they could still have something: sketched from memories of an old boyfriend, they seemed naively dramatic; John-and-Yoko meeting Kabuki. It made her queasy to consider petitioning Myron now with anything suggesting sex. She thought *Oh hell*, wrapped and mailed the originals, swearing hereafter to purge herself of the accursed hopeful impulse—a stupid, stupid reflex, like pulling at slot machines.

Somehow Teresa knew it went against all rules to demand *Why why why why won't you take my stuff?* She knew that in Myron's mind her offerings were locked in a separate, antiseptic room, one of those labs where you manipulated things from an adjacent room by sticking your hands into gloves sewn into the wall. But a deeper apprehension whispered to her his true verdict: *Your work is not good enough. Never, ever good enough.*

Teresa talked hard to herself against this sinking, damned sensation. Her work *was* good. For God's sake, at least sometimes it was. She'd sold paintings, had encouraging letters. She told herself to dismiss him: she'd find her way. Yet he was a highly placed arbiter, the validating, conferring eye. She began to wonder whether she were going a little mad.

It was an evening in early winter when Myron phoned to tell Teresa he had dropped by a small opening in downtown Denver, starring a new up-and-comer from New York: Marla Rifkin. "Ah yes," Teresa said. Teresa knew of Marla from the reviews, of course, and she knew that Marla had done a series of hotly sexual photographs.

"She's quite beautiful," Myron noted, in his "tut tut, it looks like rain" voice. "Aha," Teresa answered—*Beautiful? Beautiful apropos of exactly what? What was the educated rejoinder here?*— nearly giddy with preposterousness, noticing a pressure behind her eyes. Perhaps at last a circle was closing, or maybe a *Titanic* sinking: the final visible section of the crippled ship dropping vertically, swiftly below the horizon. "And how was her work?" Teresa asked. "Oh, it was all right," Myron answered, a code Teresa knew meant *competent but unremarkable.* He continued in his trademark tone, a disaffection so bored it could scarcely muster the energy of outright dislike. *I know he's in there somewhere,* Teresa thought, dazed. *It's all a ruse, a fancy ruse,* she thought; *he's as capable of falseness, of duplicity, of fear of the wrong step, as me. As anyone.* He wants zero risk, and nobody dares challenge him. *I know you're in there,* she thought furiously.

"It seems to me that no one these days is doing anything daring, or substantive," Myron was saying. "It all seems so small, hashings of the artists' little circles. No one's *about* anything anymore," he sniffed.

Was this deliberate? Either way it was a clear message; a pointed refutation.

Teresa felt the implication's sting like a whip's tip at her cheek.

Teresa hung up, turned off the lights, and crept into bed with all her clothes on. The room was cold; she yanked the quilts to her ears, balled herself up and put a pillow over her eyes, trying to fuse with the worn cotton sheets she pressed against. She could always go live with Amy, in Racine. They had a basement bedroom, carpeted, with a rocking chair. She'd wear a lot of flannel, work in a bookshop. Paint landscapes in watercolors.

That night, Teresa had a dream: Myron was entering his gallery late, secretly, locking the door behind him. He advanced in the dusty track lighting to the first painting that routinely adorned his showroom, a dark, cocktail-lounge version of *Dejeuner sur l'Herbe*—and climbed into it as if it were an open window. Once inside, Teresa saw Myron suddenly wearing brilliant clothing like the painting's nightclub denizens, his hair slicked back with pomade. He began disporting himself in a lurid, cocky way with the characters in the painting, making raunchy noises and gestures. He pawed at people and oozed his arms around them. Cigarettes and lighters flourished like fans and batons in the raucousness—Teresa could hear and smell it—drinks flashed gold and silver, clinking crystal and cigarette tips spangled the dim tableau. One young man's shirt fell short of his naked buttocks, and his testicles hung slightly visibly in front. Teresa stared. The remade Myron darted about, agitated, excited. He was grasping, horny, lewd with the men as well as with the women. He danced twitchily. His voice was higher. He was a dandy.

When Teresa woke before dawn she rose at once from her bed, put on soft sweatclothes, and slipped out the front door to begin running along the streets in the foggy dark. Breathing in the damp silence, looking up to watch pinprick stars pass across the apertures in the mist, looking back down to watch deliberate puffs of her own breath.

She thought of nothing at first but the streetlights' curdled sheen on the wet pavement. Then the message came into her like a transmission from a sympathetic prompter on a faraway planet: *What if he is a curator of lives.* When she heard it she clasped to the words and held them; held them hard as she ran until they began to melt their meaning into her; soon she felt something lift away like a densely spun net. She panted home in the pearling dawn, lighter, not needing to know more.

She would have at least an hour before she'd need to leave for the office, and she wanted to sketch the preliminary design now, while it was fresh in mind. She had a canvas of about the right size already stretched and primed for it—for the portrait that had been forming so long, a life-sized portrait of a man and woman having dinner. The man would be nude, of course. It would be important to get the postures right.

She was three-quarters finished with it when Myron's call of formal acceptance came. On behalf of the Pyramid Gallery, he would take the erotic pen-and-inks. They had, he said, "an energy." They would be mounted with other works for next fall. Myron added, with a strange, hollow chuckle, that he would now "have to give up" his "fantasy sex life." It would take Teresa days to realize that he believed the inks depicted current events: that is, herself with a preferred—and presumably, extraordinary— lover.

It was the last time he ever phoned her.

Green Fruit

Nathan had returned from his vacation abroad bearing all the earmarks of a most familiar problem. The girl was French, gorgeous, and half his age.

Somber, agitated, he'd sat at our table and eaten Hank's experimental salmon in pastry crust with hardly a fraction of his usual interest. Nathan liked food; he ate well and often, and he carried the extra pounds in what I considered an attractive, even lovable way. I looked sharply at his face as he told his story. It was baffled, inward.

Her name was Geneviève. Jzhahn-*vyehv*. She had met him outside an Ivo Pogarelich concert in Amsterdam. She had only paused to examine the advertising poster, but Nathan struck up a conversation, somehow persuading her of his own expertise as a guide. Nathan was a composer who taught music theory at the conservatory here in town. But in Amsterdam he might've easily been taken for a native Nederlander. Nathan was a dead ringer for a Rembrandt subject: rosy, self-ironic intelligence glinting in his eyes, shining hair hanging in boyish planks. He always kissed me right on the lips when we greeted, the brotherly intimacy a consolation.

For my part, I have always dated men who were my peers. And when I fell in love six years ago—at a dinner with friends—Hank was no exception. We have no children; our friends' children are mostly grown. Technically I know I should accept them as adults, but it's odd—they still engage me as kids, still staggeringly naive, faces so smooth and unconscious they seem embryonic buds. Lately I have tried to recall my own awarenesses—or lack of them —at twenty-one. I had traveled and worked many jobs by then, but blindly, enclosed in a thousand boxes of my own devising.

Morose, agonized about weight and beauty and love, I postured, dreamed, despised phoniness and compromise in all their sly forms, and pined for true understanding. I wouldn't now be able to stand that girl.

Hank and I have talked about it. We feel pretty much the same as we felt, say, at thirty-two, except that we are crisscrossed with more lines, grow tireder on warm afternoons, and if there's time and no one looking, dearly crave a nap. Making the bed together, the urge to fall down upon the smooth, cool material and lose consciousness is so strong we look at each other and burst out laughing. This sudden, overwhelming desire to sleep comes on like an injected drug; moves us in a haze toward the bedroom as we call out, "Just going to lie down for a few minutes"—and sink in seconds to the bottom of a heavy, dark sea, warm and insensible. We waken thickly from these afternoon spells, and it takes a few beats to remember anything. Our gravest unspoken fear, I suppose, is that it is a tiny rehearsal.

Occasionally we're dismayed to see hair silvering in the bathroom mirror. Tweezing my eyebrows in morning light, I sometimes see a face that frightens me. *"Wow,"* I murmur, staring it down as frankly as I can for half a minute. I think then of the baby photo of that same face peering over her father's shoulder, soft eyes mildly quizzical in the camera. (How many selves, how many faces since then!) I've studied Hank's childhood snapshots too; his joyful smile, sweet skin. I wonder if we imagine a spark might leap from the photograph back into us if we look hard enough.

But both of us would insist it's precisely the same spirit as animates us. Hank—he's a publicity hack for city hall—loves community theater and gardening, and little weekend getaway tours. I love my novels and magazines—of course it's tough keeping up with reading in the piddly lunch hour given a typesetter. We live in a pretty, leafy town that sprang up as a commuter bedroom, lately spreading now to form a suburb along a major highway that leads to Canada. It suits us. When two people have lived through enough, they start to feel kind of proprietary about simple pleasures. Hank adores barbecuing in summer. I feel happiest riding a bike along a creek-side path where red-wing blackbirds swoop, and egrets stand motionless in the shallow water like long white treble clefs. It smells of wild anise and roses.

The days follow one another like a strummed chord.

Hank and Nathan became friends years ago through proximity; their homes just a few blocks apart, their tastes parallel: rotisserie meats, imported beer, basketball. Both have had uneasy histories with women. I am pleased to have broken Hank's difficult streak—a few bumps, but I have come to trust that he is happy with me. But Nathan has persisted, at intervals, in pursuing very young, beautiful women. He meets them at the conservatory or in concerts or cafés. What follows his initial fascination, his invitations to coffee or a meal or music, has always been the same. He pours his concern into the pretty young one, becomes an expert on her, tries to help her do what he sees she values—ceramics, scuba lessons, llama farming, drive-through espresso stands. The women suffer Nate's attentions nervously, as they might an odd uncle's. He buys them groceries, takes them to jazz clubs, museums, picnics in the country. Yet if he so much as pats a shoulder, they stiffen and turn on him with a scolding about limits. What grieves me most is that these girls—and let's be realistic, they are girls; they can vote and have babies but they could be my friends' daughters, still asking for help with the rent—what grieves me is how they never show a flicker of curiosity about Nate: what he does (his brave, thoughtful music), where he comes from (Maine), what he likes (hiking, movies, affection). They may or may not remember to thank him for his help. They *endure* Nathan as a temporary means, a paying escort with whom they can feel taught, admired, and safe. Then they go away—infatuated with other, younger men who are better looking and who disdain them.

I am too shy to look Nathan in the eye and plead: *What on earth can you be thinking of.* We are only on teasing terms, not yet close enough that I might confront him so intimately. His best

friend is Hank, not me; his choice of companions still technically none of my business. Though I had heard about several earlier misalliances, and though he occasionally brought over rental
movies like *Claire's Knee,* I had not properly understood that this
might be Nathan's penchant—what the French call a taste for
fruit vert.

Then Nate was sitting at our dinner table telling us about
Geneviève: the estranged family, the former beau who would not
answer her letters, ambitions to quit her small, dull French town
for America. Nate told us these things with pressing disquiet, as
if to make us grasp that hers was a situation requiring gravest attention. Afterward, amid the empty plates and glasses, Nate ap-
pended his description to murmur, "She's twenty-two." Perhaps
he wanted to prepare me for the photos he was fishing from his
wallet.

I kept my face blank as I rose from my chair and came to stand
at his shoulder. I leaned away a moment to switch on the kitchen
light; dusk was turning the air a deepening blue; that sweet coolness released by the earth outside seeped through the window
screens. The breeze made the Japanese maple shift and sigh;
crickets were starting up. Geneviève glowed from the photo. Tall,
lean, no makeup, clear skin with the lightest sprinkle of freckles,
freshness of a teen magazine cover. Her hair was dark blonde,
her brows and lashes dark. Lengthy as she was, she still looked
to be a growing child; she could have been Hank's and my
daughter, shambling to the breakfast table in sweats, grumbling
about the milk being gone. Nate gazed pridefully at the photos
alongside us as if he had hatched her. Hank, too, stood to peer
over Nathan's other shoulder. After a pause he turned away to
clear the dishes, saying quietly, "She's very beautiful." To my surprise, this stung me briefly.

I moved back across the kitchen to lean against the cool coun-
tertop, propping my elbows behind me, and stared at Nate.
When I was small, Saturday morning cartoons often depicted
two hungry characters marooned on an island; each would
briefly eye the other and envision a steaming roast turkey. I

stared at Nathan and watched him shimmer briefly into something I had never considered. My mind slowly composed the caption: *Drawn to young girls.* The sensation was one of floating backward, the image of the person you believed you knew, receding. I felt lonely, and ashamed.

In Amsterdam, he told us, Nathan had invited Geneviève to come stay with him at his home in America during spring break. He would show her the countryside, take her to concerts; she could relax and not worry about her assorted private vexations. He told us all this in a tone of almost hasty irritability, a deliberate offhandedness you would use to imply that anyone decent would unthinkingly have done the same. A sort of personal Red Cross, a mercy project.

Nate must have gone a bit batty preparing for her. At first he insisted to Hank that he would visit no one while Geneviève was with him. But we knew he spoke no French; he would go stir-crazy after a week of chaperoning. We also knew that we were perhaps the only people in town to whom Nathan might dare show the girl. The conservatory administrators would frown on it, and the school was the only social venue besides us and the all-night coffee shops in town. I have a little French. How could we demur?

We found ourselves seated in a German restaurant listening to baroque guitar, glancing around at semiabstract, semigood oil paintings, smelling rich meats broil. Patrons laughed throatily and tended their handsome children with confident cheer. The place strained to create coziness; in fact a too-hot hearth was blazing. Hank and Nate scanned the long, laminated menus, absorbed in their serious choices, while I tried to keep Geneviève entertained.

She had come to the front door of the house hovering behind him as if for cover. But she was taller than Nate, and so loomed like a half-glimpsed shadow. I welcomed her as if she were a long-lost niece. Led her into the kitchen, put a glass of wine in her hand.

She was exquisite, but barely out of childhood. Dark sweater over a white, crisp-collared shirt, dark jeans, walking boots, long legs. Nose a bit large, lending her face the softness of a pony's. Faintest scent of a delicate soap. She was nearly paralyzed with shyness. Her voice was soft, breathy as Marilyn Monroe's, her English hesitant and heavily accented. From somewhere, like a rabbit levitating snowy-clean from the center of a muddy pond, emerged my best habits of French. Gently I led her back to her native language in a question-and-answer volley with all the energy I could summon. She warmed, cautiously.

"Well then." I leaned forward, balancing my chin in my hand, elbow on crossed knee. I wondered how I appeared to her. I wore a straight black skirt and dark green blouse, black hose and low heels. Could I be her mother, the woman who still put her up and gave her money and fed and worried over her? "Tell me all about how you met Nate, and whether he pleases you, and if he does not, why not, and if he does, why," I said. I said it with a twinkle, meaning partly to be funny, but she looked at me in real alarm.

"Oh! But the French are very private [*très secret*]!" she said. She looked imploring. I tried to reassure her. The two men of course missed all this, talking with each other for intervals, then looking over and listening to us in silence. I saw she was far more comfortable in French. Inwardly I girded myself: I had a long, gymnastic evening before me. But if the girl could hardly speak English, what could Nate have been hoping for?

She told me of meeting Nate in front of the Pogarelich concert, and how—she said this with perfect, innocent clarity—she herself had very little technical understanding of the music: it seemed harmless to allow Nate to squire her about, to concerts and clubs, explaining things to her. They went from one scene to the next, and it was very *agréable*. She could have been describing a municipal library she had chosen to sample, which she had found a pleasant (inexpensive) way to pass time. She was locked in the natural assumption that the world moves for her and longs to serve her because that is merely and entirely a young girl's due.

Good Lord, I thought. I must have been this way once.

In the restaurant I asked about life in her industrial town. It boasted a small business college where, she thought vaguely, she might undertake a degree. The students hung out in bars and cafés arguing economics, truth, and destiny, flirting, sulking, and smoking around the clock. I remembered Paris and could perfectly picture these exertions: the murmur, the pallor and hollowed-out eyes, the jeans as rumpled, the hair as clumped and straggly as it had been when these lanky young ghouls tumbled from bed straight out the door to the brasserie. The air almost impenetrable with blue, exhaled smoke.

I had to work to keep her engaged. She seemed to generate few questions or comments of her own; perhaps her difficulty with English discouraged it. The men ordered big entrées and steins of lager. She ordered a salad, sipped a glass of dry white. She told me she was appalled by the huge portions in American restaurants. Abashed, I glanced down: I had ordered lamb. It arrived thick as a woodblock. My body felt heavy, my clothes tight, and a light film of perspiration played over my neck and cheeks and upper lip. I saw with irritation that Hank was twinkling when he spoke to Geneviève. He joked about buying all the paintings in the place. She squinted and cocked her head, confused. I grew more annoyed that besides having to draw her out I would also be compelled to explain him to her—with a sideways glance, short shake of the head and quick *tsk*—that she should brush aside his show-offy quips. *The translator,* I thought with a tiny, hard lump of panic, *becomes invisible,* a comforting valet who stands slightly back of the actual players, murmuring protocol into their ears.

By the time we walked to the car I was exhausted. She asked to smoke. Nathan—who never smokes—raced like a frightened Mafia flunky to hold the match to her Gauloise, then to his own. We stood around awhile staring at the few distant stars, while I wondered how long my aching throat might get a rest. Nathan wanted to linger back at our house. He was probably exhausted too. We drove home in silence.

When more wine had made the rounds in our living room—

the men seated beside each other on one couch, me beside Geneviève on the other, like debating teams—a strange momentum gathered. Since the girl initiated nothing, the rest of us began in unison, as if on cue, to pour ourselves over the girl. We took turns performing, singing and tootling like separate little instruments, joking and filibustering and stumping awkwardly in alternating languages, each deprecating and elbowing and dismissing the other. Jostling, jumbling for attention, we could have been three clowns tumbling in a sawdust ring before her. I saw with horror that we were actually competing, each leaning toward the girl with tremendous gravity and fixing her dark-lashed gaze with ours, conspiratorial. It became a mission to gain her private approval, to provoke a smile, a laugh, to kindle the light of comprehension in her lovely dark eyes—to glimpse the white teeth, hear the high, breathy voice express faintest interest: these were the treasures, the grail, and each of us strove to get there first.

I could have felt superior to the men except that I was doing it too. Fully aware of it, watching myself do it with all my might. Remembering at the same time how I had once been the object of such fawning—how I'd been puzzled and vaguely repelled by it. Yet none of us could stop. It was as if we three believed the child's beauty a thing apart from her—as if that beauty knew something, could confer something. Beauty became the Pope, and three adults in their forties begged for its blessing, for their lives to be made whole by a shy French schoolgirl.

Poor Geneviève, trapped inside her pretty container, the rest of us hanging before her like curious fish staring in, eyes bugged, mouths gaping. Choose me! No, me! Me!

Geneviève left Nathan at the end of the week. He would not speak of it to me. I had to learn through Hank that Nate went home dazed and sullen after the three-hour drive from the airport. He had spent a great deal of money on the girl, waited on her, put hundreds of miles on his car taking her about, and she had offered but the vaguest thanks as he took her hand and pecked her on each cheek at the Duty Free entrance, where pas-sengers made their ways to European flights. Instead, she pressed some letters into his hand and asked him to mail them for her: they were addressed to the ex-beau who had shunned her in France. It seemed she believed that if the letters arrived to this man from the United States, he would be curious enough to open them.

I have not seen Nate for a while now. Hank and I don't refer to the episode, so I do not know what Hank makes of it in his own mind. I can guess a few things. Once, when I pressed him about a similar friend's similar venture, he angrily snapped that young flesh was simply more compelling than old flesh.

Oh.

I could accuse myself of gloating over Nathan's misfortune for some ugly little notion of comeuppance—because of my own age. But that doesn't somehow completely account for things. I love Nathan, or believe I do, and I believe I want his happiness. Yet if I stand back from events like a scientist or detective or space alien, the questions still prod. Why would Nate so stack the odds against himself? What could he have believed might have persuaded the girl to care? Sincerity? Money? Boredom?

Perhaps he had no idea. There are stories we begin to tell in fabulous desperation, hoping they will somehow finish themselves out just as fabulously on their own steam. It is likely that Nate may again select another young girl, whom I may or may not meet. It doesn't matter. I know who she is.

She is beyond reach; translucent composite of old dreams and centerfolds, designed to lift him awhile a little above the achingly predictable limits of things—to take him away, if only for moments, from the intolerable echo of himself.

We make our ways as best we can. And things do change.

But she will appear when he needs her to appear, just as she will evanesce—as she would, as she will, for any of us: now seen, now not—a tender rhythm, its brave, edgy regularity like the diastolic wheeze and rush of a pumping heart.

Exquisite

Hullo, sweets. It's me. No, everything's not fine. Everything's terrible. I just wanted to hear your voice. Yeah, an awful thing happened. Just when I thought it couldn't get worse. Just let me be sad on you, honey, just for a while, please? I have to say—I just want to disappear sometimes, you know? I have to say it. Yes. I know you don't like to hear that. I promise, I swear I don't like to say it. No, I won't check out, baby; I couldn't kill *you* that way, now, could I? But I have to be able to be sad on you sometimes, or I'll just blow up—and you're the only one who—you just gotta *let me,* and then forget about it, that's all. Do you believe I've just drunk an entire bottle of wine? Sauvignon blanc. From the health food store. I chose it for the highest alcohol content. Remember how I taught you? The tiny print that goes sideways up the label; highest number wins? Thirteen-point-eight, this one. Pretty good deal for six bucks. My cheeks are hot. It was organic, though, so the hangover won't be so bad. I promise. I've tried this one out before. Don't *worry* so much, kid; I'm safe in my little pad here. Got the guitar tape playing. That pretty little Catalan folk song. All scratchy; the one in the discount collection. The one that sounds like it's saying *And this is the way my story goes.* I want to dance when that song comes on, honey. I want to take a deep curtsy, the way you might for a lover, or the queen of somewhere. Move in wide arcs, rich and slow, Martha Graham, all balanced and symmetrical—no, I'm not gonna drive anywhere, sweetheart, I promise. I'm not even gonna *walk* anywhere, little sis.

Yes, a man thing. A man-disaster. This time went worse than the time before. Oh, we had a second lunch, even though he'd stood me up the one before. Why? Because when he called to apologize he was so *abject,* that's why. I could only melt, and say okay. You would've too, I swear it. Anybody would've. And then it really turned out to be heaven: Ah, God it was sweet. Lots of wine—Orvieto; pretty name?—and we talked and talked. Lord, it went on for miles. I told my office it was going to be a long one; they were fine with that. I should have taken the afternoon off and taken him home right then, is what I should have done. When it was time to go he had my coat over my shoulders before I knew what had happened. His hands so *warm,* and something more—well, like a taller Anthony Hopkins, I'd say. More hair, blonder. But his eyes. Ultramarine, I swear it. So pure, so clear; color of—color of the water off the Marquesas, okay? Or one of our very, very best cleary marbles—remember? We put the marbles in shoe-box houses; cut the holes for doors and windows. Made families of them. And the clearies were the beautiful daughters, weren't they? I think they were. Anyway, his eyes. Right through me. Right through my clothes. Right through my—of *course* I knew he was married! But the way he was acting and talking, you would swear it was not—not an *object.* He said the most beautiful things. Things I would never—I just don't know anymore what that *means,* when people are married, you know? I didn't know what to do. I don't want to fuck up anybody's life, I swear to you, honey; swear to God—but I could use a little *relief* sometimes, you know? Remember that quote out of *Fiddler*—"even a poor tailor deserves some happiness"?

Don't think I don't know how it looks: your older sister grim as Eeyore. Sad as a fucking basset hound. And you on your third husband with a houseful of kids. Yes. *Yes* I had lovers the equivalent of husbands—yes, okay, four of them; but people never— hey. Do you remember when we were driving back from *Fiddler,* and we were in Daddy's old car, and the steering came off in my hands? Can you believe how we were screaming then, zooming down the freeway home, the steering wheel sitting there in my hands like somebody's hamburger? What did I do, sweetie? Tell me quick; I can't remember. That's right. I stuck it back on. And it worked! Craziness. Then when we got home and told Daddy, the way his poor face went slack? I bet he wished he were making more than a teacher's salary so he could buy us each brand new cars, each of us. 'Course, Ella probably didn't care. Do stepmothers really, ever? Maybe she wished we'd been wiped out. No, I guess I don't mean that. But it was fine anyway, how it worked out, inheriting the little Volkswagen and all. Poor Daddy. God bless him, huh. Bless our pop. Sometimes I want to talk to him still so much it hurts. Fifty-three's so fucking young. Fifty-three's prime time. Guys run for president older than that. You, too? What do you want to ask him about? Sex, right? Of course sex, and labor unions, and—do you have dreams like mine, where he shows up and explains very calmly that he's fine, but he can only visit a little while? And then you go to hold him and he's really real, and you can smell that wonderful man-smell against his chest, cherry pipe tobacco and man-sweat, and you cry and cry, and wake up crying? Well, I'm not surprised. I always knew we were telepathic. We should submit ourselves to science—how long, tell me, have I been telling you that?

Know what I'll never forget? When you said you saw Daddy looking out from the baby's face. It happened, right? In the grocery store that day? How the baby's eyes held the light of Daddy's eyes, and it froze you? There was Joey sitting in the baby seat of the grocery cart, fat and gorgeous—such an *equable* little beach ball, that one—and all of a sudden the way he looked at you? And you knew it was Daddy looking at you from in there, clear as a bell? I'll never forget it, what you told me. You said to Daddy—out loud in the grocery store—looking into the baby's face: "I'm doing the best I can with these kids, Daddy; I really am." And you know it's true, sweetheart. How can you resist thinking how proud he'd be of those three little boys? I think it all the time. Each of their faces kind of a rescrambled version of his own. Might as well tell him, huh, darlin'. Whether he's in there or not.

Yeah, the guy from the restaurant finally came over. He made me wait a long time, though. And just when I'd be ready to give up, he'd call again, to say he'd be later. I was a wreck. I'd zoomed home early that day, just to get ready for him. I took a long bath, and used the apple shampoo that smells so heavenly when your hair dries, and I had fresh fruit in the kitchen, flowers, wine, the whole bit. I even got rid of all the dusty old plants and put brand new ones all around. About time, huh. It really was pretty, honey, I promise the place never looked so nice; you'd have been amazed. But ho, was I nervous. Terrified. Heart *attack*. Couldn't think. Couldn't read. I could only keep the television blasting. My mind was making all that white noise, you know? Like the car ignition turning over and over without catching. Na *nah* na na *nah* na na *nah*. Coughing and choking and never catching. If I let myself think about being with him, my heart wanted to come out my chest. I promise.

And then what? Well, he finally called the last minute of the last hour, when I had started to feel kind of cold all over. I couldn't stand it—I was about to leave the apartment. For where? Anywhere. I can't stand writhing on a pin like that; like some impaled bug. He'd known I was waiting all that time for him, and my heart was really about to burst by that point. So when he called I screamed into the phone at him, that he was messing with my head. To my amazement, he yelled back! Something about being scared. This might sound nuts to you, but that melted me. Because it was truth, and you know how it melts you when a man tells the truth that way—it was so brave, to say he was scared. Then after what felt like a hundred more hours he finally came up my stairs—what a queer feeling, seeing this lovely man, whom I've only seen in restaurants and offices, finally coming up my landing. And I took him by the hand, and there it all was again: so *warm*. The whole business. Incredible voltage, still there. Very there. My mind began to roar, and we embraced, and I caught a glimpse of us in the mirror together—my head against his chest—and it seemed nice, you know? The way we looked together. It seemed better than all right. Then he fled to the can, and I poured us some wine—I think I even had the presence of mind to unplug the phone. And it seemed, in spite of how scared he was, like everything was possible then. That's all I could think: it was possible, and it would somehow be all right.

We sat on the couch, and I put on the most beautiful guitar music I own. The Catalan song was on there. I lit candles, and then we were kissing, and off the couch and onto the floor, and I felt like the last woman on earth. He was saying and doing the most astonishing things. I knew he would be the most powerful and imaginative lover I might ever know. He had ideas. Ways he had imagined it. Different *rooms* of it. He gave me these teasing little tastes, with his words, and his movements. His kisses were like—swift attacks; very deep, lush—and then gone, before I could give back the same way. I cannot tell you the things he said—no, sweetheart, I really can't; not even you—except they were frighteningly hot, frighteningly beautiful. You just have to believe me. It was like standing at the edge of a thunderous falls, with the ozone spray wafting up. But here's where it got nuts. He would not let me undress, and he would not let it go further than the kind of urgent pressing and groping we suffered in high school. He said, "We both know it's wrong for me to be here." He said, "It could easily become an obsession." He said, "I am conditioned to feel this guilt." Nothing I could say could persuade him. Not even the notion that it was all of a piece—the first kiss, all the words, making love. No, he was having none of it. And so we were locked in this I-will-but-he-can't marathon, a stalemate, insects caught in amber. There were long moments where I was stretched out on the floor looking up at him, adoring and ripe and ready as any woman on this earth, and there he was over me, looking and looking into my face, as if he were trying to crack a code. It was all in him—yet he was locked. Madness. Like nothing I've ever known.

Suddenly, it was over. He said, "I'm going to leave now, and I want you to be all right with that." And when I turned my face away—thickness balling up in my throat—he said, "Give us a smile now." I was dumbfounded. Incredulous. I managed to speak, in the queerest flattest voice—I hardly knew it as my own.

"Why?" I said. And he said, "Because it's such a beautiful smile."
I thought, *My God. Who the fuck do you think you are?* Somehow
I formed words, and I spoke them: "Why do you go so far, and
no further? Just to see what I felt like?" And he turned his face
away very fast, and while it was turned away, his voice got louder. Let me just see if I can get this right. He said: "It's not as simple as that. It's about finding out that you can still feel that way
for someone, and that someone can still feel that way about
you." I'm paraphrasing it. I'm not getting it quite right. But that
was the essence of it. He looked away from me the whole time
he spoke. And then I was sick. I'd been a lab animal; a controlled
experiment. I murmured: "Well they can, and they do." And I got
to my feet. Walked him downstairs.

One thing more—something I'm ashamed to tell you. At the
bottom of the stairwell, in the dark, I pulled off my silk top, and
my bra. I had to place his hands on me, because you could not
see your own hand in that dark. He seemed to be thunderstruck
a moment. Then he kissed me and kind of bit me a little. Everywhere. Unbelievable sweetness, the way that makes your eyes
roll back and lose sight, the way I was certain it would be—all
this in pitch blackness, at the bottom of the stairwell—and he
was saying again and again: "You are exquisite. You are exquisite."

And then he was gone. I felt around in the dark for my shirt,
and my bra, and then clutching them I walked back up the stairs,
slowly. Naked to the waist. Numb. No idea of anything. Listen
to me. I knew at that moment he was taking long steps on the
street, my street, through the night air, through the cold still air
of my street, to his car. *And I knew the coldness of the air was sweet
to him.* Do you follow? I knew he was breathing deep of it, im-
measurably deep, and that his heart was calming fast. And I
knew by the time he got home, that heart of his would be
soothed and light and peaceful. He would fix himself a glass of
something, go to bed with a book, sleep like a child. And next
day he would be crisp and vivacious; an extra lilt in his step. And
what does that make me then—can you tell me that? Can you?

I would just like you to know that it is not *salutary,* to find a man perceives you as a contagious disease. It is not a *good thing* to watch a man watching you as if you were a black hole making sucking noises. I am still a good woman, still a beautiful woman —aren't I? No, it's good for me to cry, sweetheart. It would be bad *not* to cry.

I know less and less. I swear it. I wish I were a dog. Then somebody just *pets* you. Pets you and pets you. And you don't *displace* anything. You don't knock the stuffing out of somebody's holy equation. You don't disrupt a goddamned *teacup.*

Yes. I should come see the kids. Let me tell you something. If I let myself, when I just think of their *faces,* I go crazy. I can't stand it. I can't stand the idea that those faces will sooner or later have to see all this. Worse. They'll have to *become* this at some point, do you see? All the gory garbage of it. Already they're cutting deals—Lord, they're cutting the deals so early now. But when the sex gets mixed up in it, it's finished. Over. It's all wrong, and it stays wrong forever.

What? What's he doing? Putting a piece of cookie in his ear? No, I'll wait. Go ahead and tend him. Sweet pea—*every day,* he does that? Yes, I know very well what it's making you remember. No. I do; I really do. The years in Honolulu, when you came to visit, right? You brought the oldest over when he was brand new, and we thought he was the Son of God because he was your first. Where were we: the grocery store again, wasn't it. Seems like everything happens to us there. And how did it go—we had a plumeria we'd picked. That's right. Those lovely creamy flowers like oversized jasmine, pink staining white, out of the park in Manoa. Lush Manoa. We'd put Max on the swings in the park. And the mountains of Oahu all blue-green around us, with those piles of silver clouds like whipping cream, scudding by so fast in the ocean wind, and us, Momma and Auntie, pushing Max on the swing in our swimsuits. And then the plumeria flower we were carrying disappeared while we were cruising through the grocery store. And all of a sudden we noticed it was gone, and both our hearts just stopped right then with fear. And there was little Max riding along in his grocery cart baby seat, so mild and agreeable, staring at us. And you were staring back at him. And then it came to you. Because you're the Momma. Somehow, suddenly, you figured it out—calm and cool you were, even though he was the Son of God. And you got the tweezers out of my purse, and gently, gently grasped up with them inside his little baby nostril.

And out came the plumeria, pink-on-white, perfectly preserved, petals blooming open in flower-ballet as it emerged, a speeded-up film, a Disney documentary. And Max's amazement—his stone-pure amazement at the emerging flower—and at how we were laughing, honey. How he looked at us, blinked a moment, and then how he grinned, delighted to have authored such a mighty fine trick. And the way we were laughing so hard by then, tears streaming down, both of us staggering and gasping against the cart, falling down laughing onto the cool linoleum of the grocery store, the baby blinking and grinning at both of us like he was accepting an Academy Award.

Ah, sweetheart. All of a sudden I'm so tired, kid. Maybe I can finally sleep a little. That's something, isn't it, to be able to sleep again. Yes. Yes, I guess I'll drive up soon. I miss the kids, I really do. Sure, I promise. I promise I'll come. It's good to have a plan, isn't it. It's good to have a plan.

The Guardian

Boyd Evers was born in Boulder, Colorado, and his oldest memories are of his father walking him as a toddler to the center of a little bridge over a stream, in thawing winter.

The sky was slate; hills and trees frozen deep in white cream, and the sound of melting snow like soft bells. His father, Hal, was very tall, a bomber pilot and doctor who'd decided to practice psychiatry after the war. He would stoop low to hold Boyd's hand as he and Boyd dropped broken bits of sticks they had gathered into the dark stream below. Then the two would hasten from that side of the bridge to the opposite railing as fast as Boyd's chunky legs could move him, to scan the tinkling water until father and son could spot the sticks they'd dropped, floating along on the gentle current like a lost armada.

The sight thrilled Boyd to his soul. Something about seeing a thing and then seeing it again—still itself, recognizable, continuing as it had begun—struck him as miraculous. "Na-gain!" he would cry to his father, who would draw more sticks from his pocket as they crossed back over to the other railing. He never tired of the game, which his father called "Pooh Sticks."

Boyd had no guile from the minute he was born. A fleshy, happy baby, his eyes shone with belief, and from the start he did everything he could to please. A black-and-white photo he's kept shows him as a toddler presenting a rusted old piece of iron pipe to his beautiful mother, Elaine. She leans delightedly toward him with the careless ease of a movie actress, long legs crossed and bunched to one side, cigarette dangling from a slack hand as she ducks low to meet Boyd's gaze, smiling across the photo at him. Her brunette hair is pinned in loose waves from an intelligent, genial face. How could Boyd not be dazzled? His mother and father were tall and glamorous, their days heady with mysterious purpose. Boyd remembers a kitchen painted in fashionable Chinese red and black lacquer, dinners on cruise ships with sparkly glass catching light, cocktail parties where lush noises and smells mingled.

They gave Boyd a baby brother whom Boyd did not begrudge, Dickie, with hair fine as white duck down and eyes the blue of winter lakes. Boyd helped look after his little brother, bringing his mother clean diapers, teaching the baby to speak and walk, recruiting him early into childhood games of cowboys and war; and when Hal moved the family to an exclusive neighborhood outside Honolulu, they plunged together into the topaz-blue spell of surfing and bodysurfing. Family albums show the boys in matching pajama sets before TV trays laid with Cokes and hamburgers; Christmas trees with glass-tube candles bubbling a dark red liquid Boyd loved—they made an agreeable soft murmur like an aquarium pump. A velvety back lawn, framed in palms, sloped straight out to sea. Birthday luaus, and new surfboards shiny as candy.

Then somewhere inside all that Elaine became sick, and grew sicker. One day she went to the hospital. Boyd remembers being taken with his brother to wave up at her from the grass below as she stood at her window. He still doesn't know why they were not allowed into her room. The day came at school when the principal called six-year-old Boyd out of class to his office.

"You need to go home," said the principal simply. He looked embarrassed and sad. Boyd doesn't remember much else about that day. There is a long blank patch in his memory just there, like the spidery blotches dancing on-screen when the film runs out in the projectionist's booth, a ratcheting white hole that gestures frantically before the next images fill it—and he cannot now recall who took him home, where his father was, how he and Dickie ate or slept, whether they continued to go to school or stayed home with a baby-sitter. But Elaine was gone, and the photos from that time show two boys with wan faces who seem to be trying hard to remember something they had suddenly, inexplicably forgot.

Nellie King had been Hal's secretary since the Colorado days, and she agreed to move to Hawaii with the family to continue to work for him. Boyd believes that Nellie and his mother got on well—he has a vague image of the two women laughing together—but he was very young then, and as years overlay his senses he grows less certain. He is sure, however, that Nellie at once became auntie to him and Dickie, greeting them with affection and talking seriously with them about their lives. Nellie let Boyd punch the keys on her typewriter and found pieces of candy and toys for the brothers when they visited the office. Her gifts on birthdays and Christmases, as far back as Boyd can catalog, were always brilliantly practical; all seemed to contain a message of durability. Deluxe Swiss army knives, sturdy canvas backpacks, flannel shirts. Extra-long-life flashlights. Lined deerskin gloves and a pair of heavy, warm woolen socks when Boyd went off to college in New England. (He still has the socks and thinks of Nellie when he puts them on.) Like his parents, Nellie stood very tall. Boyd remembers her long torso and limbs sheathed in simple suits and modest dresses hemmed below the knee, her hair clipped neatly short and her face noble under heavy brows, like an aristocrat's profile on a coin. Quiet as she was, Nellie seemed to exude a restrained elegance, the kind of deliberate, thoughtful attention that would befit a foreign attaché; it calmed people. Boyd remembers her sitting on the bed next to him—not just beside it—when he was covered with the itching sores of chicken pox, her long back angled toward him, large gray eyes watchful as she read to him from Jack London. "Well, Mr. Bumbly,"—her nickname for him, from a story Boyd fancied—"ready for the next installment?" Boyd always nodded vigorously, his eyes fixed on her face. Her deep voice carried a watery waver, like her namesake Eleanor Roosevelt's, that soothed him.

Not long after Elaine died, Hal put a most unusual proposition to Boyd and Dickie. He had soon begun dating—Boyd could never later clarify to himself *how* soon, and after a few minutes of deliberating would always brush away the clouded feeling with annoyance—a redhead named Margaret, a Honolulu debutante who seemed to Boyd at that time to travel in a glistening mist of regal clothing and perfume. Her eyebrows had been shaved off and slender brown lines drawn on; her eyelids powdered lavender, her voice and gestures large, operatic. Boyd was confused by Margaret, but his father seemed to want him to like her. So he tried. Both boys were still moving through days in the groggy state of children whose mothers have dropped away, clinging to a routine they somehow hoped (with repetition) would give them back any feeling of normalcy—when Boyd's father sat them down.

"I've decided to pick a new mommy for you," Hal said. Boyd can't recall where they were when Hal called this meeting; maybe in his office. It's possible he and Dickie sat on the other side of Hal's desk, like clients. "The choice is between Margaret and Nellie. I thought I would ask each of you boys to vote, and I'll add my vote to yours."

Boyd and Dickie stared at their father. Maybe this was the way all men picked new wives. Boyd does not remember how long he and his brother deliberated, whether they compared thoughts, nor exactly when they gave their opinions to their father. But he remembers that he, Boyd, chose Nellie. Dickie, who would later become something of a womanizer, chose Margaret. And then their father chose Margaret, breaking the tie. A fancy wedding followed, thoroughly written up in the society pages. Then everything went on as before.

Only not quite. Margaret Evers hated her husband's longtime secretary instinctively, and all her married life waged wrathful war against Nellie. No one knows whether Hal told Margaret of the election he had held with his sons, or how his boys had chosen. But Margaret was a woman of honed territoriality. She had captured a handsome, eligible widower in that city of limited social options; she meant to fortify her holdings. Though Nellie lived a separate life and saw other friends at lectures and concerts, the library, the beach—she struck observers as an isolated figure, and her daily proximity to Hal was unavoidable. Margaret would aim acrid comments at Nellie when she joined the family (at Hal's invitation) for dinners or drinks, and more than once Boyd remembers Nellie finally sighing, "Oh, Margaret!" after a particularly poison-tipped remark. Yet sigh was all Nellie ever did. Not even in an angry or self-pitying or put-upon way. Just an exasperated sigh, the way you would with a tantruming child.

Where was Hal during these scenes? What did he think? Boyd still can't be sure. Perhaps Hal heard out the two women in amused silence, the way Picasso languidly watched his mistresses fight over him. Perhaps he scolded Margaret. Perhaps he feigned ignorance and went about his business. But as Boyd grew, he saw the wretched difficulty Margaret was giving Nellie; surely his father was seeing it, too.

At first Margaret presided in the new household in the style she had planned (coached and goaded in these arts almost from childhood by her mother, a strict society matron). She dressed and made up like a Dior model, shopped for gowns to accentuate her neat waist and green eyes. (Hal paid the bills with wry stoicism; his wife was still an avid sexual partner; the price, he reasoned, had to show up somewhere.) She had the sprawling oceanfront house enlarged, adding a sewing room for her embroidery. She threw parties in those first years for Honolulu gentry: politicians, university deans, businessmen (cane, pineapple, shipping) and their wives. Live jazz piano, fresh flowers; everybody piled with leis—the ocean-moist evening air floated with scents of pikake and tuberose, of grilled meats, crab, and shrimp—all the delicious pupu people could hold, offered on platters by servers in white aprons. Nellie, gracious and alert—one of the few single women—always impressed the guests. Liquor flowed. Hal had long advised his boys of the best ways to navigate these adult rituals though they were scarcely past childhood, and Boyd's memory still reverberates with many of those sayings, uttered in Hal's basso growl:

"Do only that which will enhance your cause."

"We're barely out of the trees." (As a species, Hal meant.)

"Drink just to reach the edge of pleasure, then balance yourself there."

Boyd and Dickie heard and watched it all. They dressed up and smiled and passed pupu platters and ducked off to watch television or finish homework or, on weekends, cast themselves mindlessly into the green-blue march of waves off their own backyard. Again and again they would funnel full length—one arm outstretched straight before them, hand a tight slicing rudder along the salty wall of water, until their eyes, narrowed and misted, swam red.

After a couple of years Margaret Evers began to badger her husband for a baby. It was part of her due, she argued, and at last Hal relented. An infant with pale blue eyes and ash-blond corkscrew curls was born, Petey. His older brothers, then perhaps eleven and thirteen, loved him lavishly. The photographs show them pulling the curly haired baby in wagons, propping him before birthday cakes, following him on the lawn as he takes first steps pushing a toy mower. But somehow at just this point, Margaret persuaded Hal that though they were well-behaved and cheerful, the elder Evers brothers needed the discipline and seasoning of prep school. There doesn't seem to have been room for discussion, at least none that Boyd can now recall. Photos from this period show an empty-eyed pair of young men in dark jackets, white shirts, and short pants sitting open-legged on their own packed suitcases at Honolulu International, elbows on knees, hands clasped loosely in space before them, as if having just given up on prayer. Boyd was bound for a secluded academy high in the upcountry forests of an outer island; Dickie for one in the dry hills of Palo Alto, California.

Perhaps it was then that Boyd's face began to manifest a certain wariness, though his eagerness to please was still discernible. He was tall now, and though handsome with his late mother's dark, movie-star features (resembling a young Tyrone Power), he was self-conscious and shy. Nellie had insisted, against Margaret's wishes, on coming to see the boys off at the airport, and at the last moment she pressed a couple of wrapped parcels on each of them, which turned out to be initialed leather toilet kits and fountain pens with prestamped postcards, so they could easily write her.

She wore a peach sundress with a full skirt, and flat sandals, pulling her sunglasses away as she approached. Her big gray eyes were glossy as she knelt before each seated boy for an embrace. Boyd inhaled her clean scent—Maja soap, he would learn much later. Hal had his hands in his pockets; he kept glancing around as if there were something he needed to take care of. Margaret stood by, chic pocketbook dangling from folded arms, while Nellie crouched before each boy as if performing a religious rite, locking first Dickie, then Boyd, for long moments in embrace. "The next installment," she whispered when she hugged Boyd, and he nodded as his throat closed, dropping his gaze to the concrete floor. Tears in front of Hal were unacceptable. Nellie rose quickly and stepped back.

"Let's roll, fellows." Hal clapped each of his elder sons on the shoulder with one hand and shook their hands with the other, probably offering another hearty aphorism that Boyd can no longer remember. Margaret stationed herself before them by turns and pressed a European-style *mwa* on each cheek—and the years of separation began. Of course the two came back for holidays, and they found that they did not especially miss Margaret or even their father. But they dearly missed their little brother, who effectively grew up without them.

Through prep school and college Boyd remembered to write Nellie, and she wrote back faithfully with island news, jokes, descriptions of Petey's antics, the crowds at Boyd's favorite surfing spots. She never forgot birthdays, often tucking small gifts into the mail—a couple of excellent novels for Boyd; for Dickie (a budding singer and pianist), albums by his favorite musicians. Boyd felt they were missing the lives they should have had, as the brothers grew into men away from home.

Dickie dropped from the foreground then, traveling, skiing, waiting tables, singing in nightclub lounges. Petey became a darkly serious young man, formed in the tight frame of his

mother's overprotection and his father's terse pessimism—grow-
ly pronouncements about the venality of men. Yet Hal's practice
was thriving, expanding by reputation to include politicians, so-
cialites, entertainers who paid high fees. When Boyd considers it
now, it seems mysterious that his father should have so reviled
people, since at very least their faith in his skills gave him such
a luxurious living.

Boyd knew from his father's telling that when Hal was a little
boy in Nebraska, he'd had a football he'd loved obsessively, a gift
from a player passing through town, during a parade. Smiling,
the young man had handed it to little Hal—who stood trans-
fixed—right there in the street, as if passing him a grail. And one
day soon after this Hal's mother, a woman pinched and bitter
with the hardship of her life—had chosen to punish Hal for
some overlooked chore by burning the football in the fireplace
before his eyes. The incident throbs in Boyd's mind; he imagines
it might well echo through all the rest of a man's life. Yet Hal had
also once explained to Boyd that he became a psychiatrist after
the war because he'd hoped it could help the men he'd seen,
whose minds had been shattered by shellshock. Even when Boyd
himself had begun to discover the complex dismay of loneliness
inside a marriage, he always assumed that his father drew from
some larger knowledge on the matter—hidden away. Knowledge that might in time be revealed to Boyd—perhaps as a gong
of revelation when Boyd was older, or maybe as a kind of seep-
age, time-released with visits home.

After college Petey enlisted, as if to atone for them all, as an
orderly in a California hospital for the mentally disturbed, and
announced he meant to make a career in that realm. Boyd was
married, straight out of college, to a tiny, nervous woman who
assumed he could protect her—an innocent mistake it took him
ten years to undo. (When Dickie gave the toast at the wedding,
in a tiny church near Jaffrey, New Hampshire, Boyd began to
weep and kept weeping as if his heart would break; unable to
stop.) He joined the army and with his frightened young wife

made homes at a succession of bases in various parts of the American mainland. But Nellie King never forgot him and wrote him loyally and fondly wherever he was.

Boyd kept in dutiful touch with his brothers, and in young adulthood they reunited uneasily at home each Christmas, during which time Hal and Dickie especially (juggling girlfriends and creditors) would drink hard. Margaret had begun to grow stout, swelling everywhere as if an air pump had been inserted into each section of her—an alarming effect, as if she might at any moment simply lift off like a dirigible. She had taken to wearing floor-length muumuus. Her face, once the arch magazine model's, puffed now with fatty flesh at the eyes and jowls, and her arms seemed to Boyd (though he would rather have died than express such a thing) like two raw baby suckling pigs joined at the faint seam of each elbow. Still, she made sure the muumuus were of rich fabric, that she was daubed with expensive cologne; her hair was done weekly and her face made up heavily; gold pearl chains draped where wrists and neck had been. The boys treated her with deferential care. They washed the cars and weeded; carried heavy things, ran difficult errands. Yet no matter what they did, Margaret was dour. She developed mysterious ailments and injuries for which many costly trips were made to local specialists. Everything hurt or bothered her in some morally aggravating way, and much conversation and activity was spent trying to correct the offenses—objects out of place, air conditioner at the wrong setting, the gardener's having butchered the hedges. The changes in Margaret seemed oddly arbitrary to Boyd, almost imposed, he thought. (He thought of Hawaiian curses, stories of people being "prayed to death" who needed only suspect such a curse was aimed at them to give up and expire.) Hal attended his unhappy wife with grim formality—then disappeared into his den, where he kept an array of pipes and aromatic tobaccos, a superior sound system, and floor-to-ceiling shelves filled with his own cases and books. No one was to knock when Hal's door was shut.

Nellie, whom Margaret still took pains to exclude from as

many Evers gatherings as possible, had on the other hand aged well. Her skin may have become lined, her hair and eyebrows peppered, her gray eyes filming with cataracts (which would later require operations) owlish behind thickened lenses. But she carried herself with the same grave dignity; the same erect long back, steadfastly running Hal's office, silently enduring Margaret's ugly snubs—all gentle concern for the grown boys, for the doings of the Evers clan, like some quiet guardian from another world.

Boyd finally obtained a divorce from his neurasthenic wife (she disappeared into a sheltering dynasty of communal Quakers) and has lived with a number of women since. He makes a striking housemate for awhile—strong, smiling, eager—but eventually things go sour; he angers them because he is so kind and reasonable, so unambitious, and so sad. They scream at him in furies they cannot themselves account for. He packs his few things into his camper truck and moves to a new cabin, relieved he has always resisted the temptation to remarry. He listens to his old albums, rereads his favorite novels, and plants a vegetable garden out back, a few marijuana seedlings punched into the dark soil if there's privacy. He prowls the secondhand stores and buys tuna sandwiches from the tiny grocery for dinner, with a beer.

Dickie found work playing backup for studio recording sessions, a life that fed him a steady diet of exciting drugs, which got expensive and then dangerous and finally gave way, as the sessions dwindled, to the simpler, legal fix of alcohol; now he's mostly let go of the music, except to pluck a favorite tune on a guitar when he's alone. A stream of younger roommates is always cycling through his old country house in the horse pastures outside Palo Alto, enough to pay his cut of rent and utilities. He hikes, sees movies, fixes omelets, and tries to amuse the latest in a long series of women, this one a real estate agent who for some reason doesn't mind his reliance on drink, commencing at about four each afternoon—he can claim some control with the rule, nothing before four—growing louder with evening, regressing to tears on occasion, finally surrendering to sleep in late hours.

Neither Boyd nor Dickie has ever allowed for the possibility of having children. Neither will speak of it, not even with the other.

Petey moved to Nevada with his longtime fiancée, a strangely heavy young woman named Cheryl. Both are mental hospital orderlies. They hope to save money, marry, and have a baby in a few years.

Margaret has gotten tireder, crankier, and fatter, and Hal is ill, very ill, with mouth and throat cancer from all the pipe smoking. He has been moved to the hospital, where Margaret fusses and frets about him all day long, and Hal, weakened and voiceless, can no longer speak to order her away.

Boyd is between women at the time it happens, living in a converted shed in Hilo where he is a landscape gardener. He is sleeping on his futon (it smells slightly of mildew) under his down comforter beside his overturned book when the phone rings in the early hours of a Sunday morning, a time when you know the news cannot be good.

"Boydie. Boydie. Hal is dead."

It is Dickie, telling his brother. Dickie is slurring, though it's only 10 A.M. in California.

"Oh, Dick. No," Boyd murmurs, props himself on one elbow, thick with sleep and cognizant of the vague stab that has not yet clarified to pain, sworling gases of shock already blunting his nerves at hearing the words. Boyd has been knowing that his father would not likely get better, that an end would have to come, but not this soon, not this soon, and he cannot grasp it.

"Boydie, it's worse than that. He did it himself." Dickie's voice cracks; his heavy breath whooshes into the receiver.

Boyd does not grasp this either. "What? Dickie, what are you saying? What are you telling me?"

"Boydie, he jumped. He jumped. Hal jumped from the hospital roof." Dickie is crying hard now. Boyd sits up on his futon mattress. His eyes well up with the helpless, choking sound of Dickie's crying even though the actuality is not yet taking root in him.

"Dickie, are you serious? He jumped to his death? Oh, my God, Dickie, oh, God. Tell me." Boyd, a tall man with a slight stoop now, gray threading his temples, hunches his lean form at the edge of the bed in the rainy Hilo morning, rocking, and for a flashing instant he remembers Pooh Sticks.

Three brothers flew home. They helped Margaret arrange the memorial service. They persuaded her to cremate Hal's pitiful remains. Petey especially, now a muscular young man with sandy curls, kept an arm under his mother's as she padded about the plush house in her floor-length tent-dresses, giving orders and stopping every so often to press a tissue to the corners of her eyes, dazed, gasping for breath. A tranquilizer was prescribed.

Hal had apparently thought out his escape very carefully, every step of it, like a man confined in solitary. Methodically, patiently, he'd noted the stairwell's location and the hours of least surveillance (around 3 A.M.), though it must have cost him every last fiber of effort to drag himself up. The note, penned in his cramped, pointy script, had been conspicuous on the night table. It declared that he was not interested in a "drawn-out decomposition." True to character, Hal wanted to cut to the chase, to save everyone a lot of "expense and nonsense," as he put it. In his weakened state he could not get access to enough drugs to do the job, nor, voiceless, persuade anyone to help him, so he opted for the next sure thing. Besides, he said, life at this segment "held no more surprises" for him; he was curious to find out, he said, "what might be on the other side, if there is one."

These were very typical expressions of Hal's.

Margaret was furious. Her fury burned through her and forged a manic purity of purpose: profit. She threw herself into every money-shoring tactic: attorneys, estate sales, investment futures. The property at Kailua; the apartment at Waikiki. Everything in Hal's will had been left to her, of course. Why then was Margaret so angry? Perhaps at the loss of insurance money, withheld on grounds of suicide. But Boyd knew it cut much deeper. Hal had checkmated Margaret. He had given his warden the slip; escaped her cleverly, permanently. Boyd wondered whether she regretted the whole enterprise of marrying Hal. And yet (Boyd reasoned) none of the sons had ever crossed her, and she was living so well in result. What else would Margaret have been about? Her own family was dead. Her sole hobby was embroidery. She had taken her late mother's dictum—*above all, marry well*—to its highest end. Boyd could not conceive of any other thing Margaret might rather have undertaken. This was the project she had been born to, and she had done it so well she had effected a complete coup. She was now king.

Nellie had taken a cab straight over to the house when she received the news (she could no longer drive, her eyesight failing), but Margaret claimed illness; would not speak to her. She insisted the brothers ask Nellie to leave. None of them could dissuade her. Boyd decided to call on Nellie privately, so he invented an errand in town (even distraught and sedated, Margaret monitored the brothers' itineraries) and found a pay phone. Nellie spoke slowly, asking him to come to her apartment.

It turned out to be near the one Margaret owned at Waikiki, that had been her mother's, on the Diamond Head end near the Outrigger canoe club. Monkeypod trees shaded the street, scarlet hibiscus bushes lined the walks; the ocean thudded softly behind the building. When Boyd reached Nellie's door, she opened it before he could knock. Nellie was then in her late sixties. She was wearing shaded glasses to shield her near-sightless eyes. Beyond her Boyd could make out a few old-style watercolor portraits of island children, shelves of books, a large pink conch shell on a low, hexagonal koa table.

"I can hear your steps coming, now that my eyes are going," she said with a sad smile. Her face appeared thinner, lined more deeply, and her mouth trembled slightly. With her eyes hidden it seemed to Boyd a piece of her was missing, like people in censored crime photos. Nellie stepped forward and put her arms around her old friend, her surrogate nephew, and the clean scent assailed him—Maja soap, she said—lighting up his memory like a switchboard. "Mr. Bumbly," she whispered, and Boyd's eyes filled. He followed her inside.

When Nellie died at the age of seventy-four, completely blind and succumbing at last to an assortment of ailments that had brought on pneumonia, Boyd received a thousand dollars in the mail as part of the disbursement instructed in her will. So did Dickie, now pasturing horses behind his Palo Alto farmhouse, and so did Petey, living with his plump wife and new baby boy in Las Vegas. But Boyd was the only one who made the trip back east for the funeral. He stood amid the older people he did not know (also tall, smelling of camphor and liniments and hot cereal), in a small St. Louis church: family friends who'd only known Nellie in girlhood and early youth. The minister spoke of "the peace that passeth all understanding." Boyd wore a tie. Afterward he sat politely in the reception room, at fifty-three the youngest person there; more gray flecked his temples and salted his thick brows. He drank the tea-colored coffee and ate the too-sweet cake, and tried to explain to anyone who inquired what this tall, circumspect woman had done for him, been for him during her life. It was no use; eyes hazed affably, perfunctory words blessed him, powdery hands patted his. Boyd couldn't hold it against them; she'd been away so long. Who among them could have known her? Voices murmured regrets: soft cooing, feathers stroking.

Nellie never married, you know. No children. Always lived alone. Bless her.

Among the mourners was Nellie's only sister, Anne, a woman who faintly resembled Nellie—not quite as tall, longer hair, wire-rim glasses, clear skin; a mild, sensible aspect—who had made a more conventional stand; grown children and a suburban ranch-house in Texas. It was Anne who had sent the money directed by Nellie's will. She seemed resigned but calm as Boyd pressed her dry hand with both of his, thanking her for inviting

him, and on the plane back to Hilo, he resolved to write her what
he knew. It was not so much a decision as a reflex; fervent, un-
gainly; perhaps the last thing he could seize as the lens screwed
closed, as events of the past few months began their inexorable
dissolve. *It has to be passed on*, he thought stupidly, over and
over—though he'd known enough to see it was not a thing you
spun out face to face, especially not surrounded by the conservative elderly at a funeral home in St. Louis.

*Now that I've described Nellie's part in my growing-up days and
my many lovely memories of her, I come to the difficult part—and
Anne, I apologize for this because it's likely not fair to you, but you
seemed when we met like a person who has lived a while. I'm telling
you this because somehow it seems you should know, but I'm also
telling you because I have to tell it. And though this will sound ugly, I
mean it as blandest fact: it can't finally matter very much to me how
you may take what I'm about to say. I can only try to explain it as . . .
well, a kind of duty that demands discharging. (My brother Dickie
knows, but not my youngest brother Petey. You'll soon understand.)*

*After my dad's death, when I went to see Nellie at her apartment—
I had to conceal the trip from my stepmother Margaret, who has hated Nellie for as long as I can remember—during that visit Nellie told
me of course about growing up with you in St. Louis, about going west,
answering the ad for a secretary in the Boulder newspaper, commencing work for my dad.*

*Then she told me that she and my father had been lovers from the
very first.*

*You should probably know that my father was a tall, handsome and
commanding man, his voice gruff and deep, and his work during the
war, as a doctor who volunteered to fly bombing missions, and later his
work in psychiatric techniques, made him a kind of star in those days.
He would have been in his early thirties then; Nellie a couple of years
younger than my late mother, Elaine. Almost as soon as she met him,
Nellie said, she allowed my father to seduce her, and over the years she
cooperated in supplying him with every manner of sex he could invent
or desire, with various props and costumes and aids, taking care—*

great lengths—to conceal any trace of their activities from my mother, from all of us boys, and of course, later, from my dad's second wife,
Margaret. Much of this would have had to take place in our home, in
my father's main office. None of us knew. It went on straight through
his life, behind everything else that was happening, until he was tak-
en to the hospital with throat cancer. Nellie would have been in her
late sixties by then, Dad his early seventies.

Nellie recounted these facts to me as if they were as natural and unremarkable as brushing your teeth. I must have been speechless. Then
she asked me, as a favor, to go back to Hal's office and bring her any
memento of him. I went home numb, and (telling Margaret I was
cleaning, my heart pounding for fear she would come upon me at it)
began to go through my dad's desk drawers and files. This was still very
soon after he died; no one had yet tackled the dismantling of his office. In his desk, in the far-back of a file drawer, I found a collection
of the apparatus Nellie had described: kinds of things I had never seen.
Pictures, clothing, tools. One by one I lifted out these objects and held
them in my hands.

I couldn't at first decide how to remove them safely—it would have
killed Margaret to learn of them. I finally placed them in an old canvas military duffel from my father's coat closet. Then, rummaging
more, I found an ashtray with the old Lurline cruise line motif em-
blazoned on, from the fifties. I stuffed this in my jacket pocket like a
jewel thief, nervous to the point of feeling faint, and seizing the duffel, thrusting some few scattered papers into the wastebasket as evidence of my cleaning efforts, raced away.

I dropped the duffel bag in a public trash bin.

When I brought the ashtray to Nellie, her face fell. "I had hoped for
something more personal," she said, and I felt like a messenger in war
who has fumbled his mission. Back I went, and again with pounding
heart and under the ruse of tidying, plunged into my father's effects.
This time I found, with a lot of rifling, a little book in which he had
scribbled. I fetched it back to Nellie, who clasped it and looked up
gratefully at me. It was full of his handwriting, and he had kept it in
his breast pocket, "over his heart." That was how she put it, and I saw
I had somehow finally compensated the woman who, though he gave

her a comfortable living and a generous retirement, had been left out
of Hal's will; whose true part in his life, all his living days, had been
submerged.

I have thought about it. It seems Margaret must always have known
at some level, and so her lifelong hatred of Nellie was not exactly un-
founded, and yet that cannot in my mind seem to excuse it. Nor does
Nellie's subterfuge make her less to me, exactly. But the Nellie I be-
lieved I knew doesn't fit with this—this thing she opted into. For me
it is like pressing on a library panel and feeling it give way to open
onto a dungeon. Though she expressed no regret to me, her situation
couldn't have been without pain. It makes them all more confused in
my vision; I doubt now that I understood, or understand, much of any-
thing about any of them. Anything at all.

When he thinks about it anymore—because as with all else,
the impact of such knowledge fades with time—Boyd tells himself that things happen in waves, like the sets he learned to spot
floating offshore, to suck in a lungful of air and dive under again
and again, listening to the muted roar of the break above him
until he could rise through the bubbling sand and salt to emerge,
gasp for breath, reconnoiter.

Sometimes when he is turning the soil, shoveling over the
sandy loam and leaves (dark and crumbly, already half-becoming
earth), he stops and shakes his sweating head suddenly, like a
horse with a gnat in its ear. How far, he thinks. How far it had
come from those pearly photos, wry grins, sweet baby faces, a
thousand cocktails, a thousand toasts. Boyd imagines now—
when he thinks about it at all anymore—that when the human
event is done, no other shoe need necessarily fall. We just wish
it would; a childhood reflex, maybe: a longing for balance, for
comeuppance, for the story to end well.

He plants his shovel in the humid afternoon. Clouds are
piled, white and guileless. Behind them, or in them, is what we
are, where we go. In some ways, he thinks, it's a kind of mercy:
people perpetrate things, bizarre or sad or noble, and then they
die one day, and there is no coda, no punchline, no vaudeville

snare-drum punctuation. There may be a witness or two for awhile, a friend, a grown child, alone with their untellables. But don't expect a last word. There is no other shoe to fall. Boyd shakes his head, picks up the shovel, inhales, slices it with a metallic stab into the ground.

When the Universe
Was Young

The evening, the evening: Maxfield Parrish blue deepening to ink, behind silhouettes of palms crowding oaks, firs, willows— a Northern California vision Jean has always loved, along with the way the air cools and sharpens and fills with exhalations of the very young spring. They are bathing and dressing, Jean and Jake, preparing to drive to a birthday dinner for Jake's boy, Sam. Sam is turning nine and for the occasion has decided to offer his favorite food to his father and his father's girlfriend, fettuccine "fixed a certain way," he calls it with great thoughtfulness. He means, the way his mother makes it. Jean and Jake see Sam every other weekend; they love him helplessly. He is an old little soul, Jean likes to think.

She has given herself and Sam lots of time to make their way toward each other since they met five years ago. Sam was playing with two neighbor kids in Jake's front room. He'd said hello, blushing, and disappeared back to his friends. It was the first night she'd visited Jake for dinner, and the first night she'd kissed him, quickly, after he'd told her—leaning back against the kitchen stove, arms crossed over his chest, gazing at her in a calm, brave, cut-to-the-chase way—told her that he frankly had a relationship with her in mind, if she were thinking of that too. She had been flabbergasted but must have nodded stunned agreement, and he'd smiled and pulled her toward him. And just at the full flower of that brief kiss, soft and loose and fruity, melting into all manner of possibility, they'd heard the back door slam as young Sam tore in after his next pleasure. And they had bounced apart, startled, a little shy.

Jean feels that she is luckier than most in the matter of inheriting a part-time child because Sam's nature is sweet, and his ethics are those of his father's: Have Better Fun Constantly. "Jake *likes* pleasure," she still mocks him occasionally, fondly, every time he dances a little jig or whoops, anticipating his favorite savory roast or leg of lamb, marinated in olive oil and rosemary and garlic slivers, baked with round red potatoes, or unpopping a bottle of the excellent (and still-reasonable) cabernet, straight from the shining green wine country where they live.

Jean and Jake will drive to the home of Sam's mother Connie, and the man she married last year, an electrical engineer whose income and disposition most closely matched the goals she'd written on her Lifeplan Workbook Wish List. Connie had followed its instructions to the letter, meditating quietly on the items she'd written, reading the list aloud cross-legged on her living room carpet, then burning it in a dish, watching the threads of charred paper curl, mentally willing her wishes into the fulfillment department of a loving and bountiful cosmos. The man who surfaced soon enough, Ralph, turned out to live across the street, and it also turned out that his ex-wife was dating Connie's ex-husband. The community is that small, and in this place and time these sorts of recombinings are not just inevitable, but ordinary.

Jake was a tall, eager building contractor who'd lost a wife quite young, to leukemia, and, rebounding like many early widowers (long before Jean), had made the rounds of available women in the town. He had seen a lot of Connie, a divorcée who was already rearing a young daughter. Jake made steady, good money; they were both lonely. The town is like any rural town in which opportunities for making one's living are limited, as are the number of marriageable men. The two tried awhile to make a life with baby Sam; finally their disparities prevailed—though as years pass, the cobwebbing over that history thickens and the fondness born of habit, and relief, overlays it.

When Jean began seeing Jake, little Sam was shy but friendly, and Jean had resolved to take the high road with the boy: She was honest and attentive without fawning. She began to notice what he liked, and to realize that he was unusual as he climbed the years because he had not yet grown corrupt in the horrible manner she had seen other boys do. A light appears in their eyes that seems kindled by the devil, Jean thinks—not the light of boyish mischief, but of a cynical new understanding; something about the way adults trade goods for behavior, mouthing all the niceties but mainly wanting peace, and willing to pay for it— that was what kids finally caught on to, at about age nine. Their response was naturally to milk this exchange for everything they could. Not all kids, but many. Jean has always felt exposed when she sees that sneering light in young eyes, because she knows there is truth in their discovery.

Sam likes getting things, no question. He's a chunky boy but lengthening perceptibly now, copper-haired and freckled, cute as a cornflakes ad, who eats and eats if a thing tastes good, blissfully unselfconscious, until he suddenly realizes he is too full. But Sam also contains an oddly adult instinct for kindness and justice, big and floppy as these notions may be; a genuine wish that people be happy. Jean has watched him enough now to recognize it. Sam has stopped his mother and teenaged sister (now safely off to boarding school in Switzerland) in the midst of their fights, himself in tears, sobbing that they must quit fighting or they would "ruin the day." He lectures Jake about smoking cigars, exceeding the speed limit, wearing a helmet on his bike. Sometimes these moral policings worry Jean, because she has heard that children who take on adult concerns become—oh, what is it—codependent or some damn such, when they're grown. Still, Jean holds to the idea that Sam is simply a wise soul in a growing boy's body, and the part of him that likes to eat hot dogs, play Little League and computer games, the part that cries when he is scared or frustrated, seems right for his age in years.

Jean loves watching Sam with Jake, because they laugh hysterically, and because they are so alike it makes Jake rueful. Sam seems the perfect medicine for Jake, the boomerang door-prize forcing him to experience exactly his own effect on others—his own cheerful hedonism. Sam is not yet too embarrassed to throw his arms around his father and kiss him, which floods Jake with rabid tenderness. Once Jake told her that if he were informed he had to saw off a testicle in order to save Sam, he would have to quietly call out for someone to fetch the saw.

Jean wipes the steam off the mirror and towels off roughly. The pure backlit blue of dusk is seeping through the window's frosted glass. Grabbing the comb, she tugs it through the dark mass of wet curls, staring down her own clouded reflection. Though she can feel awkward at such gatherings, tonight's will make Sam glad. He loves having both sets of parents be friendly together. That prospect, together with anticipating his favorite food and birthday presents, must be floating him ten feet up just now. Jean both envies and feels wistful about Sam, thinking, *It only gets harder from here.*

Before the mirror Jean steps into a long, ranchy dress, jade green with western studs at the shoulders; sprays cologne at her throat and fluffs vaguely at her drying curls. She peers closer. Threads of white now space evenly through, concentrated enough at the top front quadrant to become a vague streak—but Jake says he does not mind, and she has no heart to commence the whole coloring business. All the energy these projects need! If she didn't have to work, perhaps she'd have that energy. She'd have her nails done weekly and shop for cunning ensembles. She could look like Connie, who often came to the door in a new haircut of fresh dark winy color, trim from her workout, wearing a smart folk-art outfit and a smooth, calm face, having just had a massage at the Shamanic Healing Center. Did everything between men and women devolve to money? Money and energy. Connie had money now, and true to her wish list it had taken care of a whole level of things, leaving her free to worry about a whole different level of things; a fierceness for order. Jake, on the other hand, liked pleasure.

Jean's face in the mirror, she sees, reflects too faithfully its real fatigue. Working full-time, commuting on a bus—you wore it all

in your forties. She sighs. You wore everything you did, smack
on the kisser. As the work week progresses, Jake says, she ages
years; then by Sunday evening her face rolls back to youthful
again, like a reset odometer. Is one thing nobler than the other,
she wonders dully: full-time homemaker, full-time office grunt?
She shakes her head, tired.

Sam greets them at his mother's door, throwing it open before
they can knock.

"Hap-py birthday!" Jean cries, and stoops a little as he
emerges and wraps his arms around her. Jake stands behind,
laughing, as Jean kisses Sam's hair, which is the color of a new
penny. She holds his shoulders a moment and examines his face.
He seems relaxed. She had worried that he would be inducted
into a lot of fretful preparation tonight, but she sees that he's
been given the green light to run loose. *Good: kid certainly should
be*, she is thinking.

Sam backs up and flings himself at his father, who holds him,
grinning, "Hey, Buster Brown." They follow him into the split-
level home, a large, thickly carpeted affair: plush, beige-and-
cream, unblemished as a real estate model. Across the room, presents lay unwrapped: books, toys, and a giant inflated medicine
ball, candy-apple red of a gum-ball machine. Sam pounces on it
to show Jean and Jake how it works; on his back, on his belly,
bouncing madly. The vivid red ball seems a prop in a magazine
shoot.

"Ralph is outside, getting a surprise present ready," Sam pants,
sprawled from a tumble off the ball.

"Ah!" Jean answers, with a waggle of eyebrows. Sam is intoxicated. Jean tries to feel for how she must appear to him against
this more familiar backdrop. In his mother's house she feels
more like a polite visitor; an auntie with furtive affection privi-
leges. Two years ago on Christmas Day Sam had begun to cry at
the prospect of having to leave his newly opened gifts at his
mother's in order to join Jean and Jake to drive to their tradi-

tional meal with friends. He hadn't wanted to hurt his father's feelings either, and his tears had been tears of frustration. It cannot be easy for the child, Jean thinks; not easy for any child who goes back and forth between homes and parents, packing a bag every other weekend in some sort of permanent tourism of his own life. Yet it was the way kids lived now. And Sam knew he was beloved. His sturdy equability reassured them all: true harm had been avoided—more deliberately really; thwarted.

Voices and clatter draw them toward the kitchen, where women are talking. One is petite, about Jean's age, in a sweater and blue jeans, with delicate features and what appear to be outsized breasts looming up like a centerfold's, talking to Connie at the stove. Connie looks up from many steaming pots with a slight frown. She is a slender woman whose face reflects many of her son's appealing features—pert nose, freckles. She lets Jean buss her on the cheek; the two women oddly complementary. Jean works an office job, doesn't cook, sees housewifery as a lifetime of drives to the store. Connie devotes herself full-time to the household, to the rearing of her children. "People-making," she calls it. "The most important job in the world."

"Of all days for it, someone came to the house today to tell us the water would be cut off all afternoon!" Connie is saying to Jean.

"Of course," Jean sympathizes. "It's a law of nature. These things are mandated—the thing you least need," she adds uselessly, somewhat desperate to make herself clear.

Connie ignores this, stirring the enormous pasta brew. "We just now got the food on," she mutters, cranking the wooden spoon. Jean's attempts at wit have flumped, a bunch of flowers in an overheated room. "Have some wine," Connie says without looking up.

"Wonderful, thanks," Jean nearly gasps her relief, spotting the bottles on the counter. Good chardonnays, merlots. They're definitely celebrating here. Opalescent wide-mouth glasses gleam alongside. She uncorks and begins pouring. When Jean had first begun seeing Jake, Connie had kept her distance. After Connie began to see that Jean was not a bimbo or a shrew, and that she cared enough for Sam to firmly hold him by the pant legs when he insisted on leaning out her second-story apartment window to drop a football to Jake below on the sidewalk—Connie had softened toward Jean; even written her a thank-you note. Then Ralph had entered her picture, and things went their rapid way. (During the early, uncertain part of it, Sam had astonished Jean by reflecting, with the patient, genial gravity of some seasoned director of international relations: "Jean, you *need* to meet my mother.")

Behind her in the noise and steam Jake is making small talk with his son's mother, something both are good at now. Jean has watched often enough to know, without looking, how they look together: Connie's automatic fondness for Jake, a certain annoyed amusement. Jake is all studied cheer. He has learned to listen well to Connie; they trade advice—the pledge between the two parents always, thank heaven, *minimize difficulty for Sam.*

It's Jake addressing her now. "Jeanie, meet Blythe, the friend I've told you about." He disappears. Jean is shaking the delicate hand—slim, barely-there hand—of the woman with breasts rising like parade-floats under the gray cashmere sweater. Her blonde hair curls in on itself at the tips, mid-collarbone. Blythe blinks gray-blue eyes, speaks in low, cultured tones. She is machine-tanned a burnished gold. "I'm so glad to meet you— heard so many nice things."

"Thanks," Jean says, not remembering anything Jake may have said about this woman. Her memory's occasional lapses distress her—that queer smack into a wide, blank screen where moments before, a clearly identifiable object or idea had been. Yet something is stirring uneasily at the back of her brain. "And what is your connection to the gang here tonight," Jean asks politely.

"I baby-sat Sam," Blythe smiles. "I've known them ever since."

It seems Blythe is a real estate sales agent. She was *there* for Connie during the early years. Jean hates the way this word is

used, reproaching by its very pitch: she was *there* for her—you
weren't.

"Ah," says Jean. More significantly: "Aha." Where were the use-
ful, polite words, Jean wondered. The necessary noises. We all
use them; we're all complicit. We're all liars, she thought, smiling mistily at Blythe.

They are called to the long dinner table. At the head, Connie
and her husband, Ralph. Beside Connie, Blythe; across from
Blythe, Connie's grandfather, a florid, bent creature who is very
old and almost insensible. At the other end, Sam insists on sitting on his brilliant cherry medicine ball, bouncing it under his
bottom with zeal for the novelty. Connie objects briefly but sees
his heart is set; demurs. Sam has instructed Jake to sit on one side
of him and Jean to sit next to him on the other, because, he says
—in his euphoria, directly to Jean—"Because I love you."

Jean stops a moment in her automatic movements to be seated. That word has never been used between her and Sam, though
Sam is very fond of calling it out to his father and his mother,
long after he has been tucked in for the night, or through the car
window to them as he is being driven away. "Love you!" Again
and again. "Love you!" It has tugged at her, as if he is working
hard at lacing together the two domiciles, two worlds. And so
Jean has never presumed to use the word, waiting for a day when
it might emerge from him naturally. But that timing had always
been up to Sam. She wonders if Sam will remember he said it.
Whether she might now use it herself without exploiting or embarrassing him. Sam is a sort of agent of goodness and though
it makes no sense that he be that, it just happened. Like a visita-
tion. He's a normal kid who likes pizza and *Star Trek* and win-
ning, and who cries when he's hurt. But when he is with Jean he
chirps along unprompted, hale as a songbird. It chastens her, reminds her of ways to be in the world besides her own broodi-
ness. Sam's declaration makes Jean feel kind of crumbly, followed by a tight panic. She can't fuck up now; she can't easily
back out.

Jean has been with Jake five years. They expect to be together until they are old, though sometimes Jean makes bitter noises about filling a U-Haul with her few things and clearing off. Sometimes she hates him as only a woman can hate someone she lives with and has grown to know: every fart, every repeated dinner-table story. Yet he is heartening to see, with his dark hair and coffee eyes, and comforting to hold, smelling and tasting like vanilla custard no matter how many pork chops he eats. And Jake is kind. He buys her favorite things: earrings and tofu and spinach; Henry James novels; lemon-mineral water; Dove soap. After a time she agreed to move in with him, to the gentle suburban house she first visited, noticing the puffy pink roses and jasmine and rosemary bushes at the front door; the slanting porch with its plastic deck chairs; old fifties tiles in the bathroom. Everything softened with wear; just the right amount of shabby. A sweet old house in a sleeping town, pretty and bland as an alien's best mockup of Earthling life.

Noise and dishware, food passed around. Here at last is the famous fettuccine fixed a certain way, which turns out to be a light alfredo sauce and fine-ground black pepper. Braised green beans, also Sam's favorite, and garlic bread. Sam would live on garlic bread if permitted. Connie has instructed Jake that when Sam is with them he is not to be allowed to eat just bread. Jean and Jake let Sam be, for the most part; let him stay up for a movie or get a second bowl of frozen yogurt. He never abuses this; a tacit understanding floats among them. Sam looks like a Norman Rockwell portrait of Tom Sawyer: his green eyes bright, his skin clear. Jean can hear perfectly in her head how Sam's voice will sound when it drops to the register of a young man. She is already thinking about when he visits then. He will stoop down to kiss her, have a patchy red beard, his hair hanging in bright shingles, possibly spectacles—and he'll lean forward at the table with gigantic forearms, telling them what he likes best about the astrophysics program at Harvard. Will there be a girlfriend? It is early to say, but seems likely. He has a crush on a girl at school.

Jake gets the details at bedtime, after they read. Jean gave Sam the *Danny Dunn* series, and *Harriet the Spy*. Jake gave him Hans Christian Andersen, whose stories, he claims, get very dark and netherworldy. But he and Sam both like them fine.

Blythe is now smirking at Connie's ancient grandfather, who squints back pink and taut, inscrutable as a Buddha. Someone has slipped him a glass of the good wine he should not have. Connie raises a glass. "I want you all to know you were invited tonight because you are part of Sam's special circle, people he loves and who've helped me with him." Glasses go up. "Thank you." Clinking all round, little bell chimes. Sam loves clinking his glass of fruit nectar. Ralph clears his throat.

"A joke?" he says. All faces look over expectantly.

Ralph is a smallish man with a sober face. He has built from scratch the kingdom around them, and Jean keeps a soft, anguished feeling for him, because he is staking everything on it. She wants Ralph to have no difficulty for the remainder of his life, though he's unlike her in so many ways. Ralph is all the thoughtful virtues: steady, cautious, sensible. No sudden swoops.

"Knock, knock." Ralph.

A chorus. "Who's there?"

"Impatient cow."

Sam, duly taking his part. "Impatient c—"

"Moo," inserts Ralph quickly, with his resolute face. That face could have just ordered a cheese sandwich in a diner, or said it looked like rain tomorrow.

A stunned moment, then surprised laughter from all sides. Sam has to think about it some extra seconds, then bursts into his wicked fountain of musical laughter. When Sam laughs like that, even if you don't know what is funny, you want to. And you start laughing anyway, not even knowing why. It usually sets Jake off, which it does again this time. Jake's laugh is high-pitched and slightly insane, making the others smile and twitch nervously. Jean has watched this combustion a thousand times and enjoys it, especially when father and son are wrestling on the bed. Their bare legs and feet get jumbled and Sam's are so big they are almost interchangeable with Jake's: a four-legged demon, howling and squealing on the futon.

Blythe leans toward Jake with a wry gleam. "Jake, you really are beyond help, aren't you?" Her eyes sparkle with deliberate intimacy. Jean stares. Jake shrugs, still helpless with cackling, teary-eyed, at Sam. Blythe turns back to conversation with Connie. Jean hears them say "scars."

"What is the story with this woman?" Jean corrals Jake as he emerges from the bathroom while dishes are being cleared, marching him backward into the bathroom and shutting the door behind them. Light on. Fan. Lemon-painted walls; fake lemon air freshener. Back of Jake's head in the mirror, front of her own darkened face. "She makes no distinctions. She flirts with the old man, the married man, anything with a penis. Who is she?"

Jake's face is a masterpiece of casualness, a thing he can affect quickly. "She is the woman I told you I dated briefly, before I met Connie—the one who went to Findhorn to commune with the plants."

Dated? "Did you have sex with her?" Rushing blood, roaring ears.

"There were some interesting bits," Jake offers, as if he were comparing flavors in a spontaneous quiz about colas at the supermarket, "but no, we did not have sex."

"Jesus Christ! With those big plastic balloons?"

Jake remains nonchalant. "Those are a recent renovation," he murmurs, brows hunkered. Jean is having none of it, forcing her mind not to rove over what may have constituted "interesting bits." She did not know Jake then, she tells herself over and over, an emergency incantation as the air raid sirens wail. *She did not know anybody here, did not know the damn town existed.*

How old is Blythe?

"About your age." He is eyeing the shower curtain intently, a pattern of dark gray umbrellas with yellow handles, floating

Magritte objects. "Jeannie, we've got to get back to the party." He
moves a little. "Jean, listen. Blythe had a daughter, who—"
   "But surely at forty-seven she's gotten over penises!"
   "—*Died*. Killed in a plane crash. Jeannie, it's okay. Forget
about it." Jake worms past her, kissing her nose as an afterthought like punctuation, his face serenely featureless. It doesn't
change things, Jean thinks, though blinded a confused instant
by the news of death. Did Jake secretly wish he were with someone like Blythe? He has in fact proved loyal to Jean. At some deep
center she knows that he, like most men, would certainly *like* to
have sex with a woman like Blythe, but maintain the sense and
wit to keep the urge a fantasy. It still gives a woman sudden ver-
tigo, she thought, to recognize men diving for camouflage when
asked—the sodden silences; carefully neutralized faces. *I just
wish I knew where to be*, thinks Jean, plodding through the plush-
carpeted hallway, a little drunk. *Alice was able to dispense with
everybody*, she is thinking, the Red Queen and all her henchmen,
by exclaiming, "Why, you're nothing but a pack of cards!" As if
by catching things out at their actual size you could break a very
old spell.

   "You're just in time for the cake!" Sam is grabbing her hand
and pulling her forward, and there it is, a baseball field with nine
candles—one at each base, pitcher's mound, catcher, shortstop,
three outfields. Someone has put Beethoven's Ninth on the tape
cassette, because this too is one of Sam's favorites. The flames
throw light under Sam's soft chin and cheeks (which give off a
perspiration-clover scent when Jean kisses him that she has not
smelled since her own baby-sitting days); reflected candlelight
puts little clusters of gold in his grinning eyes. Sam has always
accepted ceremony with such happy ease it makes Jean wonder
whether he isn't some reincarnated king. He pauses significantly to fix his wish. Then he leans forward, inhales noisily, and
spews a theatrical gust of air over the icing. Some of the flames
are doused; others relight—trick candles. Scurrying, more blow-

ing, noisy laughter. Blythe is chatting up Ralph; Connie is immersed in policy-making with Jake.

Enough wine has gone down to give Jean the kind of sad reck-
lessness she thinks pointless and exhausting in drinkers—herself or anyone else. There is no belonging, really, she thinks, not
for an aging sad sack exiled late to the suburbs. *To whom can I
speak today;* she remembers the line with maudlin satisfaction. It
was an appeal—a little essay, inscribed in hieroglyphics by a
lonely Egyptian centuries ago—for someone to understand him.
A high-school teacher had taught it. Jean wanders up to the sliding glass door at the dining room's edge and peers through it, to
the vast redwood deck Ralph has built.

A telescope is out there.

The surprise present.

Ralph has caught sight of her and ducks quickly ahead of her
just as she is stepping through the sliding glass door. He turns
back to the door after she passes to slide it closed behind her,
and as the cold spring night floods against her skin like lake water, her face is pulled at once skyward by the darkness and, im-
probably stark against it, the brilliant fixture of the moon, white
and chalky and lit, so blazingly she can make out some of its spidery creases and blotches from the deck where they stand.

All thoughts dim as if turned down, obliterated in the milky
spotlight.

"Oh! What a wonderful place for watching the stars," Jean
murmurs, barely sensible of her words. "You don't have so much
city light to interfere . . . "

"There's still a fair amount," Ralph mutters, hinting it is more
than he'd like. Ralph's modesty always makes him point out the
slight imperfections in his careful arrangements, Jean marvels—
prudent and exhaustively researched and risk-resistant though
they are. He steps ahead quickly again to adjust the oversized
binoculars set upon a stand he's fashioned. He moves with doleful, self-conscious manners, making a series of practiced, gallant
adjustments for her comfort, even as he answers her exclama-

tions and questions, which are blurred a bit (she tries to eluci-
date crisply) by the abundant amounts of wine they've drunk.

Jean's heart tightens for Ralph, for something she can feel
from him tonight, something he's decided and imposed on
himself. Deferential, acceding. Even amid this kingdom he has
wrought with that same steadfast dutifulness, he is mute and shy.
It pains her between her breasts, sharply. As usual, Jean wishes
she could be the Blue Fairy from the *Pinocchio* cartoon, the beautiful blonde who materializes out of starlight through the window, glowing heavenly blue from all parts of her, who smiles ten-
derly, waving a wand that pours blue sparkly star-milk over all
the things she blesses. Jean would bless Ralph, touch her wand
under his chin, gently lift his eyes up and smooth all care from
his heart that instant.

"It's an amazing view," Jean breathes, filling her lungs with
sharp, sweet air from the surrounding firs, taking in the distant
wide black blanket of land, honey-colored lights pressed into the
far edge of it like topaz lozenges. The foreground where they
stand is drenched by the merciless blanch of white moonlight.

Glancing back through the glass door, Jean sees Connie cross
the room, carrying plates and laughing at something Blythe is
saying. Connie's laugh is frank, Jean notices; prettily so. Sam is
punchy with all the attention, sweatily racing from one to another like a hyperstimulated pup. Jake is chatting up the old
man. The "Ode to Joy" has started up. Jean wonders whether any
of them will grow curious and slide open the glass door to join
her and Ralph, but no one does, and so she feels that muscula-
ture, which readies itself for a visitor, relaxing. She turns and
steps up to the high-powered binoculars, as Ralph has beckoned
her to.

"Now, this may be too high," he says of the adjustment, stepping back, "because I've made it to fit myself." He has aimed the
big binocs at the moon, guessing correctly that she is burning to
view it first. Even as she approaches she can see the lens surfaces
flashing two hot-white coins of the image they contain.

Then Jean is seeing the surface of the moon, in that real moht of itself instead of a magazine or television or movie; bobbling a bit like a perfect reflection on a drop of water. The flat glisteny surface is crosshatched with grey mounds and hollows and scratches, with one big crater like the navel of a cantaloupe. Though tonight is not officially a full-moon night, there is sufficient meat on the sphere to make her feel she is having a momentous First. She feels absurdly tender toward Ralph, who has facilitated this gift so quickly and humbly for her. *This gift,* she thinks, and suddenly the tinny music of local earthly dramas strikes her as comic under the patient, blind white pour of moon and stars.

"They think the moon is probably a piece of the earth from the original explosion that made it," Ralph is saying quietly. "When the universe was young."

When the universe was young! Jean's wine-soaked mind drops, sudden and sickening, as she conjures a smear of light: the young universe a smear of light, untried, radiant with promise—and suddenly Jean feels sad, and oddly shamed. Here is Ralph telling her about the elements that make up the heavenly neighborhood that have bobbed there, mild and attending, since we were salamanders. Since before all the people who made the people who made her were made. And the only thing that has bound them all, for absolutely certain, was that they have looked up—starving or crying or dancing or dying—at these same teasingly familiar connect-the-dot pictures made of jewels, and wondered why they were alive, and what death actually brought.

Jean rarely thinks about the fact that her life takes place on a round planet, coated with a breathable atmosphere. She wishes she could remember that fact more, because she guesses it might make problems easier to face, given their hilarious perspective. Jean is happiest swimming laps in the local community pool, outdoors, with a kickboard pillowlike behind her head. Then she can look straight up into the sky. Buoyed by the water, no one to interfere, she can scan the expanse of it. She loves the open span of the infinite then, nothing between her eyes and limitlessness, a space that seems to bear no grudges. She has often thought she can speak then to people who are dead, like her father; it's easy to suppose the dead may live out there. She misses her father, and secretly hopes against her own practical suspicions that the Tunnel of Light people might turn out to be right —that he and her mother, who died when Jean was Sam's age, might be waiting at some metaphysical docking station when her own life leaves her.

But Jean loves Earth—at least, in its better moments. She would be afraid to leave it if someone offered her a joyride, even just a quickie around the solar system. Most people won't admit that. Most men and women swear to Jean they are eager to go look at other worlds. Little Sam already assumes that he will be traveling to a well-populated space colony or a moon tour when he's grown. Jean and Jake always nod and encourage Sam to imagine it further, and then Jean gets kind of dreamy, because she knows she'll be dead then. How will Sam remember her? Probably cursorily, but pleasantly enough. A brief picture might zip across his mind, maybe of Sunday morning with his toaster waffles popped up and Jean pouring him a smoothie of orange juice and bananas. Jake wants Sam to lean into the future, to wrap his mind around it as boldly as he can, and Jean is touched by this, though certainly she would do the same for any child of her own.

Any child of her own. Jean blinks at the pocked neon chalk in the lenses. There had been some chances for that, twenty-some years ago, and when it was clear that the men were not going to stay, she had decided she could not do it alone. This no longer hurt: She feels no residue of tragic sin, as she once did. What still makes her flinch, though, is something more terrible to Jean: That she could never find it in her to justify the world to any child she might bring into it. That in spite of all the brave poetry and music and heroes and urgencies of high school teachers, it seemed too terrible a world to represent clear-eyed to any child. She could help other people's children once they arrived, but she could never bring herself to look into the eyes of any being she might have summoned here and then say, *Well, this is it,* like some landlord waving at an unwholesome apartment rental.

Maybe Earth, Jean now muses, is figuratively about her age. Old enough to know it was cute and forgivable once, but that possibilities were narrowing. To know it would now wear whatever it did. That it could no longer get away with certain early foolishness.

"Have you looked at any stars through this yet?" Jean turns to Ralph with a kind of furious eagerness. "How about that big sparkly one over there?"

"Which one?" Ralph pivots in the direction of her gaze, instantly alert.

"That one." She points, her whole arm raised and stretched, rigid and straight as a child's, toward the biggest rhinestone in the collection, a flashy red-blue-silver-chartreuse-yellow-diamond dinner ring with fire boiling and licking from it, even to their naked eyes. When Ralph brings it into the magnifying display of the binoculars, the result shocks Jean.

A fountain of fire bubbles and streaks in every direction, flicking and sparking hot primary colors. Bolts of liquid fire; a stew of suns. As Jean gapes, unwilling to let it leave her sight for a moment, Ralph is complaining.

"This is the difficulty of a low-powered scope, you see: the atmosphere makes the image rough," he is saying.

"The best view is the one from space itself, free-floating, away from atmospheric debris and light," he says. Jean murmurs, sympathetic. She loves Ralph helplessly now, as indeed she loves the others, whom she can see without looking: swimming back and forth with their cares behind the sliding glass door like an exotic aquarium, with their deaths and breasts and jokes and squabbling.

Surely Ralph is correct. The best view of a star will always be from a pure, floating vantage point in the velvet black infinity that contains it. But as her pupils contract with the slightly pleasant pain of the brilliant invasion, his words seem to scratch, fade to a staticky frequency, tiny mewling words of a mortal man not yet lived fifty years: words that have effectively built this machine and will build others a million times better, but that now must hush. Because they might tarnish its miracle: the diamond flames splashing and foaming into her eyes, flames from something she will never know; something, perhaps—how is it people always liked to say it?—something, however dazzling, that might be long extinguished by the time its light is seen.

Boys Keep Being Born

Henry is never sure he is living. The routines have become so ingrained, so rote, he says, he calls his few hours at his lovely, precolonial home "the flip turn." He has to do certain things, he tells Melinda, like taking yoga, to remember his own body and the fact of the earth. Henry is a risk assessor for insurance companies, administering questionnaires to clients, whose answers are fed into big mainframes for some enormous firm's policy review.

Melinda is assistant to a software company on the opposite coast. She met Henry at a Chicago computer conference and immediately conceived a liking for him. They would chat in the hotel buffet line, intrigued. But since Henry already lived with a lover they settled for staying friends the way people will, on the telephone once a month. A low-budget psychic hotline.

Enough years have gone by that they can confess things they would not have dreamed of at the outset. Once, years ago when Henry had business near Melinda's city, they contrived to meet for dinner, drank some wine, and kissed afterward in Melinda's parked hatchback. But to do more than kiss would make things unworkable later, so they had desisted. The reward for desisting, interestingly, has revealed itself to be a sense of secret sanctuary, reachable only in phone calls or letters, giving the friendship a delectable charge of relief.

It has touched Melinda that, for all his fastidiousness, Henry had traveled with a carnival as a mime troupe performer when he was young, amid sweaty grifters and junk food and second-hand cars. And Henry has savored the fact that Melinda went to work for the Peace Corps in West Africa when she was the same adventurous age; that she'd stood inside the sad walls of the slaveholding prison on the island of Gorée. It had smelled, she had told him, old as centuries.

When Henry and Melinda settled back into their lives on opposite coasts she sometimes thought of their friendship as a
thin pliant underground tube, the kind light travels through in
fiber-optic demonstrations. If everything else became hopeless-
ly chaotic you could drop away temporarily and confide in the
sympathetic other, like speaking into a secret safe hole in the
earth.

For a long time lately Henry has wondered aloud to Melinda
whether he wasn't in love with his yoga teacher. He would wake
up at five o'clock to slip from bed and get dressed, feeling furtive
and mysterious in the velvety half-dark. He would drive to the
studio in his sweats and take his place at a respectful distance
from the sleepy few stretching on the shining wood floor. Henry would wince if he caught himself in the mirror. *Old,* he would
think. (Henry is a nice-looking man, Melinda reminds him, and
it's fine for men in their early forties to have silver in their hair.
Silver, or possibly snow, she reminds him: "Not *gray.*") When his
instructor appeared, a thirtyish woman in a body leotard with
russet hair in a long ponytail, his heart would quicken and his
posture lengthen. (Instantly Melinda sits up long in her chair.
She crosses her legs and tucks one heel under her bottom, the
way Henry used to tease her, when they met, was *so western:* "You
take up more space in a chair," he laughed.) While he watched
his teacher do her asanas in her pearl gray leotard, her long back
arched down between legs spread tightly and the muscles of her
calves so smoothly defined, he desired her desperately. Then he
would feel melancholy and reckless.

Melinda listens to Henry with one eyebrow cocked. She loves
Henry, loves the zigzag way they talk—*first your pet loathing, then
mine*—but he continues to get himself embroiled in these sexual slipknots of longing. Unanswerable, self-replenishing longing
that is happiest unappeased, really: Melinda knows Henry would
immediately have complaints were he to miraculously become
the yoga teacher's lover. She can picture him grimacing as he
speaks into the phone of his latest difficulties with that wry, self-
annoyed graciousness of his. Henry's plaintive tone often ends

in a question? As if to remind you he knows he is disgustingly self-immersed? Like all the other last-gasp white capitalist yuppies? But it was somehow tacitly agreed that the rules of their hotline would allow this: complaint without solvability. In fact Henry taught Melinda how to ask questions for answers, gentle questions to draw out the poison. Though something in her chest goes soft with fondness every time she listens to him bravely doubting his life, other parts of her (wrists and solar plexus) go cold when she hears him longing to fuck someone other than the woman he lives with—like every other man high to low, thinks Melinda.

Henry is titillated by the sight of women in his city during the summer. Sometimes he'll drop by a topless bar on the way home from work when he is feeling surly toward his girlfriend, Lenora, a worthy woman he has lived with many years. Lenora is serious, faithful, and often away, managing women's evening wear at a tony department store. They've been together fourteen years. Henry spends a lot of time alone in his office, at home puttering, or listening with a kind of hungry wistfulness to his friends' stories. One of these in particular Henry wants Melinda to hear today.

Something about his urgency makes Melinda not want to hear it.

"Do you have to tell me this?" she says into the phone, looking at the postcard of the Louvre tacked to the cubicle wall. Henry often calls her at work, because his time zone is three hours ahead. But though she appreciates his paying for the call it isn't easy to talk from a cubicle, a small box of gray fabric with invoices pinned to it; the calendar with its numb messages. She has to be careful of her words, of employees who may notice her in the obvious, hunched tension of sheltering a private call.

"You might be able to make something of it that I can't," Henry is saying with quick firmness she does not recognize. She has never heard him so bent on a thing. Authority. *Gets it from his work*, she thinks. *Advising. Prescribing.*

"Henry, please don't tell me this. Seriously. I'm not sure it will be good for either of us." She is ashamed to beg, to describe how an unwanted image can gobble her imagination and take up residence there, a toxic alien that will rumble and throb through her dreams for God knew how long. Forcing back the thread of queasiness that has begun snaking up, Melinda looks at her fingernails, which always break off after a certain level of growth, staring back at her jagged and blunt until she finds a nail file and the time to wield it. She needs one now. Another stupid chore. You never saw a man racing off for a nail file, unless he was a guitar player. She feels oddly twitchy. She feels like bolting.

"Just listen," Henry will not budge. "Then you can decide."

He commences the story of a friend. Call him Ray. Mid-thirties. Married to a pleasant, attractive woman of about the same age. Two small, sweet children. They have a good house upstate, and Ray commutes to an excellent job as an investment broker, with plenty of ongoing advancement. He is a boyish man—

"I know what comes next," Melinda interrupts dully, conscious already of a loose, shallowy heartbeat and a slightly panicked ache in her belly. She twists her back in both directions, then hunches again, shading her eyes.

—A boyish man who (for reasons either too well understood or too inchoate for Henry to say) is insatiably interested in sex with women other than his wife. It is all Ray talks about, and he keeps inventing schemes for meeting new women each time Henry sees him. Henry cannot help feeling drawn to Ray's aggressive hunt, as much as he is disturbed and unsettled by it. (Henry counsels his clients kindly, worries about human progress, yet by his own admission cannot bear being with anyone at all for more than two hours.)

Ray has begun finding ways to visit prostitutes, the kind who are passable-looking and well-paid. Henry says that Ray does nothing but plan feverishly for these visits, then talk about them to Henry, then plan for the next ones. Melinda tries to envision Ray. She pictures one of those square-jawed, Clark Kentish men who model crisp shirts in Sunday magazine layouts. Suddenly she remembers reading about a sex addict who would go to specialized, expensive call girls and say, "Take me to a certain level and keep me there for as long as you possibly can." She keeps thinking about *a certain level.* The moment just before a wave breaks, perhaps, or before fireworks begin to bleed darkly back into the summer night. She wonders what Ray's wife is like. She shakes her head ferociously to clear it of the sad pale image that has instantly begun to form there, a beseeching ghost. *Jesus, what a miserable business.*

Henry has momentum now. The thing is, he tells Melinda, Ray finds a woman this last time who is young and reasonable-looking, but more important—who has just a month or so before—*had a baby.*

Oh God, thinks Melinda. "Oh, God," she says.

This woman's breasts are still spurting milk, Henry explains agitatedly (*Yes. Agitatedly,* notes Melinda) and the woman is nonchalant about letting him taste some, and in the course of sex with Ray it gets all over the two of them, sticky-sour breast milk making hissy noises as their skins come apart. (*The whole room must have smelled like spit-up,* thinks Melinda.) And somehow Ray, the paying john, finds this added dimension a perk, an exotic bonus. He decides that their sex is especially rich and textured because the hooker is a brand-new nursing mother.

Melinda can hear in Henry's voice that at some level he truly believes this; that he is entranced by it, tormented by it, needful, sore. It isn't perhaps that he himself wants to copy Ray's performance, to do exactly what Ray did. It's that he wants to do *something.*

"Did this woman indicate she felt the same way Ray did?" asks Melinda. She can't avoid sounding like a cross-examining attorney, though the images writhe in her mind under a dark plaid veil, the pixilated, blotchy way things look before you puke or faint.

"I don't know," says Henry, coming suddenly to a bewildered halt in his narrative, like someone waking from a channeling session.

"Did Ray see her again?" asks Melinda, still straining to sound offhand.

"Not yet that I know of," says Henry. "But I think he means to." His voice is anxious, as if awaiting a doctor's judgment, or the interpretation of a wrenching dream.

Like my father who slept around, Melinda thinks aimlessly as she packs up to leave. She turns off the little tube of fluorescent light and takes her coat off the smooth plastic hook. Her father is dead now, but when he lived he was led around by his penis as if by a divining rod. Finally one day Melinda's mother took too many sleeping pills and Melinda and her sister were swept off to another life in another city and the years stole over the vision of her mother's death-sleep, scrunched on her stomach in bed, crumpled blue mouth—years poured over it now like layers of cloudy vinyl that people protect their carpets with: you could sort of see the colors and forms beneath, but thickly; with successive layers of years the view got blurrier.

Melinda bids her officemates good night, hoists her shoulder bag, and pushes out into a late afternoon the color of peaches. She trudges to the bus stop along the concrete beside the freeway, kicking away gravel, standing patiently in its foul exhaust to climb aboard. For some time she has dreaded this commute, but it has a special anguish going home. People are tired and smelly. There is seldom much room on board, and traffic is gridlocked. A dozen Mexican workers, already seated in the back, lean out unabashedly into the aisle to get a good look at the length of her. Melinda is a normal-sized brunette. She wears a tunic blouse, straight skirt, and sandals. When local men driving past her in the supermarket parking lot cannot closely see the forty-eight years etched in her face, they yell, "Nice ass, mama!" Melinda likes the Northern California winters best, when a long raincoat covers her like a reassuring blanket. She takes a seat and pulls open a book, trying to disappear from her viewers' lines of sight as the big vehicle roars and snorts in the bumper-to-bumper crawl, throwing her from side to side. Her shoulder bag is between her ankles.

Melinda has lived a venturesome life. She has traveled, held an amazing array of jobs. Lived with men and somehow never thought seriously about marrying any of them. Marriage embarrassed her with its costumes and formalities, the fact of referring to "the marriage" like a cement by-product of some kind. Once the zero-marriage sum worried her; then worry too simply faded. Lately, time seems to have taken on an amusing eternal quality. Outer-space time, quick-and-never; a slow wheeling of which Melinda, moving at whatever speed, is more and more aware she has been accorded the briefest, briefest slice. She finds herself now moonwalking through the strange region of not young, not a mother, not married, unlikely to marry. She will have to work until she dies. She will have good friends who'll keep an eye on her, of course; some of them women much like her. She will float toward and finally past the margins of sexual viability, and never have enough money for a face-lift.

People will be interested in what she says for a little while, warmly encouraging before turning away.

A young Mexican man also rides the bus to and from work these days, a sincere simpleton—he may be mildly retarded—living out his youth blind with horniness. Melinda has watched him sit beside any woman he sees, swiveling his head to stare full-face at her for long, oblivious moments of trying, trying but failing perpetually to understand what he is seeing. The young man speaks no English but can ask the time by pointing to his wrist. As the chosen woman automatically glances at her watch he can stare some more at her: gaping, stunned, as if he cannot saturate his eyes deeply enough. He can see her glancing down to examine the hour, hear her voice speaking to him: watch her moving arm and head, her eyes rising to his (never mind how nervously) as she tells him the time. Perhaps her cologne wafts from her as she moves.

Then the young man will ask her *"Español?"* with an upward inflection. When the woman answers no he grins a big gummy triumphant grin and begins to murmur his longing to her, confident she won't understand, so that he can say what he likes, even if in fact she is dimly comprehending, with belly-sinking horror, that he is saying *Your mouth is like a rose.* He smiles conspiratorially. *You haven't understood a thing, have you,* he gloats in Spanish with his wide gummy grin. And when he speaks you can smell his breath, which unfortunately smells like fresh shit.

Even when he sits in front of Melinda and she watches him swiveling his big head around, back and forth, scanning the women in the bus seats and calculating whom he should next sit beside, when he speaks to the young woman across the aisle (any woman who is a woman) the smell of his breath floats back through the seats to Melinda.

It makes her feel faint with hatred, then shame, and then sadness. She wriggles closer to the window, pressing her face toward occasional thin streams of fresh air pouring from between the glass panels, trying to reason with herself. The poor boy is not planning to blow up the World Trade Center, or lacing people's Tylenol with poison. But she hates the fact of him and the fact of how many more hims there are and of all the women on the poor overworked earth, young and old, who must see him, hear him, smell him, know his desire, let his desire enter them time after time as they look away and think of work to be done. Wondering why the limits of things have manifested this way. Even when she gets a job closer to home, so she won't have to see it so often, it will go on exactly the same. And boys keep being born. When trapped with these thoughts, she wishes (like all the other women have wished at some no-escape moment) that she had been born something else, somewhere else. Wishes she were a moon rock.

In the end Melinda's eyes go glazey out the window. Somehow she is still sorry for the poor stupid bastard. Sorry that finally any man, every man, is this hobbled, leering boy. Henry, her father, Ray the whoring investment broker: artist, soldier, president. Sorry, sorry, sorry. It is not only pity for these haplessly cruel creatures who must assuage a reflexive itch. It is *regret* she feels in the French sense, Melinda decides. Open hands and morose gaze straight into the petitioner's eyes. Sincere discomfort with the whole arrangement, earnest wish that the present lousy state of things be struck like a stage set and remade from scratch. A functionary's courteous complicity: Of course we all understand that things *should* be otherwise, madame. *Je regrette, madame.* Because (Melinda reasons) she still carries such a strong *sense* of the possibility of Otherwise, of a kind of parallel existence of Otherwis*eness.* The foundation for us could have been poured another way. Couldn't it?

She shrinks against the window to glimpse the simpleton's open thighs, his cowboys boots. She wishes she could make him not have been born, though she is sure his mother loves him. His mother!

The penis looks the same on them all, ironically. It dismays her with its dumb relentlessness. A mutant lily by the side of the road, she thinks. Too smooth, sickeningly heedless. Penises are like mongoloid children; all the same features irrespective of the owner. *But they cannot help being born with it.* Later, Melinda notices, women give up and admit that the whole business has always frankly quite baffled them.

Tonight, the young Mexican filled with yearning sits down next to someone behind Melinda. Actually Melinda does not know this until she hears a sharp, female voice shriek, *Please don't sit here. Anywhere but here.* Then she sees the young man jump up and try to mask his confusion by saying *Ahhh, nooo, Español?* And the woman's voice behind Melinda not stopping, trembling with anguish, with rage. *Anywhere but here,* she says again and again, her voice raw, shaking.

Melinda knows everything the woman feels and wonders should she turn around to speak. The bus tonight has just unloaded at the terminal; it is filled with empty seats, but the young man has seen his chance and planted himself beside the tired young woman who must have already experienced his awful head-swiveling appraisals and shit-smelling breath, his open thighs, the whole careful vaudeville of asking the time. And she has cracked.

As who would not, thinks Melinda with stricken admiration for the woman's courage. *What is wrong with me,* thinks Melinda, *that I would likely have sat there mute and agonized because I would have feared committing a racist, classist act?* What is wrong with Melinda is that she is the kind of woman who cannot raise her voice against a man unless pushed to the very wall—because he is some mother's baby, because once his foot had been a tiny pillow of soft and milk-fragrant silk in a warming female palm. But the woman behind her has reached that wall and her scream is furious, shredded, harsh, a cornered thing.

An hour later, Melinda steps down into the warm suburban street and begins to walk home beneath the trees, sun-shot green like stained glass. She loves the floaty relief of arriving to this street, the trees' kind bending to attend; the sound of the wind stirring them. Smells of cut grass, sharp scents of daisies, mint, fading roses. Distant barking: a whiff of someone's barbecue. Two plain-custard butterflies chase each other through the motes of late afternoon light. *Why can't I accept all of it and be done with it that way,* she wonders. *We're all just little animals.* Debating thoughts—bafflingly tireless and scornful—retort: *Because you think that to say you accept it will actually enable you to. That you will be set free of it. When really you are never free of it until you are ugly and old. Maybe not even then.*

She scoops her mail (bills, ads to the unkillable Occupant) from the little wooden box on the heat-baked porch and lets herself into the dim apartment, registering without consciousness the still, musty air that settles into empty rooms during the day. Barely stopping to see how the potted plants look—not throwing open any windows—not even noticing how many times the red light is flashing on the answering machine when she walks straight up to it. In one smooth motion she tosses the bills in a flutter to the bed, cocks one shoulder down to let her bag slide off, picks up the receiver, and dials Henry's office.

It will not do to phone him at home in the evening. She can picture a New England kind of house, deliberately spare, clean, freshly painted; capacious kitchen smelling of some heavenly dish, say with lobster in it. An elegant bowl of gardenias thoughtfully placed in the warm, pooled lamplight.

"Hello, you've reached the office of Henry Siegel. I'm away from the phone right now, but if you'll leave a detailed message I'll be sure to return your call as soon as possible."

Melinda hears in his careful tones the determination to present a calm Professional. One who professes, who represents to offer. And if she did not know him she would not also hear, just peeping its tiny sweaty edge out from behind, the tight sadness of uncertainty in Henry's voice. No one has certainty; few let on to that. Henry admits it, sometimes, a little. It makes her soften a bit with recognition—but the vision of him has already distanced itself in a dutiful reversion, as she knew it would with her premonition of his story. The image she carries of him has receded and shrunk; even his voice sounds thinner as if through a damaged line, a sputtering satellite relay. The lonely cosmos filling fast with debris.

"Henry, I have to talk to you. Please call me soon."

She will ask sympathetic questions. She will listen and speak, in a hundred ways still editing what daren't yet be told. She will gently castigate him and ask him to explain himself. Her heart may contract, but she will listen and murmur "Mm-hmm." If she keeps listening long enough, perhaps one day some silvery vision will shimmer toward her, finally making things clear. She will listen because the givens of friendship are multiply strange, and because friends are hard to find. But what she most wants to tell him, to find a way to say without saying, is *Please, please don't sit here. Anywhere but here.*

What Winter Brings

White hair, vein bursting through forehead, Bob Barker all-American regularity of features over which age has been superimposed and pulled tight, like a head-stocking of dusty cheesecloth.

These were the first impressions of the woman arriving to a party of old teachers, in a quiet northwestern suburb. She came with her husband, who was in that company still a comparatively young teacher. It was three days to Christmas, and every night of the prior week and the week ahead had been booked with obligatory appearances in the homes of his cronies, old and young. The woman used to resist these rounds, which usually regressed to shoptalk; now she believed she had made an odd peace with them, if she could only keep her mind still enough to avoid thinking where she might otherwise be—for instance, striding her former city immersed in her own silent monologues. Living on good strong coffee and the *Times*, slipping deftly from dinners and gatherings as soon as they bored her or made her too lonely. That loneliness, however, had in fact become absurdly repetitive by the time she had met her husband—years of climbing those apartment stairs (their old, oily shag carpeting) night after night, to no caring sensibility within, had seemed a steady, whispered indictment. And so she had allowed him by degrees to take her away: to this town, these friends, his own insistent quests. She loved him helplessly, but was still rather stunned to find herself a practicing member of a complacent bourgeoisie. She wore a gold camel-hair coat, matched necklace and earrings, Allure cologne. The night outside was clear, pinpricked with a few far stars, and freezing: the diamond-dust of frost reflecting window light on the lawns.

Voice astonishing, self-miked, she was noting of the character who'd at once commanded attention. He stood amidst a group of men, all old like himself. The house looked like one of those in the advertisements for life insurance—quiet, restful, mani-cured with neat front porches, lawns sentried by tall birches whose leaves cascaded, four-paned windows with drapes gath-ered and tied off on each side like theater curtains, allowing cov-etous passers-by a peep at the warm life beating within.

She let herself be drawn away from the white-haired man, into necessary small talk with the host and his wife; the getting of drinks. She glanced back at her husband, who had instantly linked into the circle of older men by the fireplace. It would fol-low that he would spot them and leap there, and she was not sor-ry to see his face lit—by firelight, and the noisy reassurance of male camaraderie. She could hear above their voices the extraor-dinary voice of the white-haired man, ringing through the room like a call to assemble for the most amazing story or song, a lev-el of amusement such as would not be found for miles in any di-rection. She heard her husband ask for a scotch. And she ac-cepted a glass of wine, watching herself select from her standard kit of evening small talk. She spoke to a tall physics professor, re-tired, who was unhappy: at once she divined that he was di-vorced—bitterness wafted from him like a scent—and she knew that he would have been even harder to converse with had he be-lieved her single. He had the habit of staring straight ahead of himself into an invisible zone for long minutes before he would answer a polite question, and she felt his utter exhaustion with whatever unspeakable absurdities had hobbled his life. There were so many advantages to arriving in tandem.

After they were all seated at dinner she was able to be near enough to the man with the white hair, to listen. He looked from one to another as he spoke, compulsively, she thought, proba-bly not seeing anyone in particular. The stream of speech that emerged from him was like nothing she had heard before: a stringing-together of long-ago events, snips of conversation, rag-tag descriptions of landscapes, people, names, vignettes—the segues were not logical yet he hopped them lightly, insistently, anecdote to anecdote, whose points were invariably lost on him once he reached the moment for exploiting them. Yet he could not stop, working his way to his stories' finales with such deliberate and voluptuous care that both he and his listeners were left somewhat bewildered at the limp inconsequence of his trailed-off conclusions. He was, in a word, giddy, yet he carried an aura of high tragedy. After a time, and from his own blithe admissions, she understood that the white-haired man was taking antidepressants. But later her husband insisted that the behavior she had witnessed had in fact been the man's personality all his life, round the clock: manic, brilliant, and sad.

He would twist with one hand at the fingertips of the other, much the way that fussy, effete academics are depicted in caricature. Yet she had never actually seen anyone do this before, and again she noted the gesture was a tic, entirely unconscious. His hands were big and lumpy at the joints, fingers and fingernails large and long; the skin over them mottled. He had been a geology teacher: those hands had hefted time-striped chunks of rock and clay. He was tall, long of limb, and wore a suit; at its middle a moderate little belly plumped his clothing. He had lived with another, well-known, now-dead male teacher for most of his campus years. He was alone now: seventy-nine years old, a living relic, fragile, semihysterical, a hyperconscious repository of all the history in the world.

Stories at the level of detail that is senile dementia, or a child's, she is thinking.

The company has been seated, and the food passed around is like its hosts, stolid, unpresuming. A ham, brussels sprouts, yams. Corn cakes. The wine is from big bottles of a jug brand, because retirement income has to be parsed with fastidious care. The white-haired man—Larry—never stops talking, and his food moves around but does not much diminish on his plate: *Driving the Amalfi coast with Doris that year, she accused me, oh when was it. The ship's captain during the storm, who told us to pull our thumbs out of our asses and get to work. What they don't tell you about Brahms, you see—*

Shut up, Larry, interjects the host at one point, calmly.

All the people he cites are dead, she is thinking. *He still believes them the important ones.*

The motions of eating have waned, and at the host's suggestion all return to the living room, where Larry is handed a piece of paper she later learns he has himself brought to the event. Without fanfare the room quiets. Larry reads first from Yeats's "Byzantium," and the woman is touched to watch her husband turn toward their host with glad looks at each of his favorite lines. She does not, unlike nearly every other person there, know "Byzantium" by heart. But she is sorely fond to see her husband still so love the lines he hears.

Then the man Larry booms a different poem.

> Come, drunks and drug-takers; come, perverts unnerved!
> Receive the laurel, given, though late, on merit; to whom
>   And wherever deserved.
> Parochial punks, trimmers, nice people, joiners true-blue,
> Get the hell out of the way of the laurel. It is deathless
>   And it isn't for you.

Everyone murmurs and laughs with pleasure, particularly at the way Larry enunciates *Get the hell out of the way,* a swaggering defiance slurring the words. The words are flung out to the air like a dish of rejected food—as if a shrewd matron emboldened by vodka had loosed the syllables throatily and extravagantly; rolling out that American *r,* sweeping clear the table of febrile clutter.

He means himself, thinks the woman. *He's the pervert unnerved.* And who is to say he is not right?

The man Larry doesn't pause long to begin a final offering, more somber from its opening notes.

> I have wept with the spring storm;
> Burned with the brutal summer.
> Now, hearing the wind and the twanging bow-strings,
> I know what winter brings.

The group listens harder this time, without the twinkly indulgence of before. Larry looks at the paper with a fatal half-smile, as if pierced clean through by an opponent's single sword thrust, and out of his mouth resounds that almost sickeningly rich voice, stentorian and heartbreaking, a self-mocking gallantry attempting nonetheless to be gay, gay in the old-fashioned sense. He breaks down midway with a kind of hearty half-laugh, half-sob.

> Goodbye, goodbye!
> There was so much to love, I could not love it all;
> I could not love it enough.
>
> Some things I overlooked, and some I could not find.
> Let the crystal clasp them
> When you drink your wine, in autumn.

The woman is full of these words, the wrenching singsong *Goodbye, goodbye!* as she steps over the host's front door threshold into the night, into the compressed, arid frieze of Christmas stars, of hard winter—a vast black box with tiniest pricks in the lid. Husband and wife step out into the night, into their car that still smells of leather and carpeting.

The woman and her husband sit in the car a few moments with their eyes full of what eyes see when rubbed too hard; black stars. They know they are the Larrys of the future: trapped inside his hapless, failing body and his hypervigilant memory. They see the objects around them disintegrating in fast-forward: the car, the clothing on their bodies, their bodies themselves. All, all is marked with the invisible infrared of a predetermined shelf life. *Why do we never say it,* she wonders.

And now, says her husband, starting the car, now we must go back to our regular lives and believe *they* are in fact the most important thing. He switches on the car's heat, and at first it blows cold air. She says little; looks out the window at the lights of the town, the moving lights of lives in cars gliding around them.

They arrive home, turn the heater on, check the answering machine; their nostrils quick with the pungency of the little fir tree they've garlanded with red tinsel; they move about, feeling for the light switches; colored foil of wrapped gifts catching the bit of light thrown from the kitchen. There are teeth to be brushed, doors to lock, something taken from the freezer for tomorrow. Bed.

He will want sex. But she clings to her husband like a sister, trying to will him to ease her desolation. *How can we live differently?* she begs, knowing with a loose rancidness in the pit of her belly she is begging for an appeasement he has no power to grant. *I don't want to join the rot, the cold, the neverness. Don't want to become it.* He strokes her body and tells her they've no choice but to live as fully as possible, and then he is distracted by her body, and wants to make love. She has no heart—has she ever? —to decline on the grounds that her brains feel about to explode. So she presses her mouth to his warm neck and thinks of a line in a book by a woman who once climbed into her mortally ill husband's hospital bed with him: *the living flesh of my husband.*

I must remember, thinks the wife.

Soon, her head against his warm chest—always smelling faintly of butterscotch—she asks her husband to explain "Byzantium." He peers oddly down his chest at her a moment; gives a short half-laugh. The poet, he tells her, finally chooses to come back as a little golden mechanical singing bird.

But with whom does the poet file this petition? thinks the wife. Or to what? There is nothing listening: only the tiny finches that land without a sound in the boughs of the plum tree alongside the yard, peering calmly at her as if by omen; only the squirrels pausing a nervous instant on the telephone line, tails luxuriously aloft behind them like plush fur balloons.

There is only the grisly, grisly news. She cannot rid her mind of the photograph in the magazine, leafed through in the supermarket checkout line, of a man chasing down another man to kill him, in a faraway third-world country where skins were dark and there was nothing to have or hope for. It was, said the caption, a religious war. A second photograph showed the man preparing to cut the throat of his already-dead victim, whose face—contorted with horror in the first photo—now looked voided, emptied of personality and horror alike, a half-deflated ball. She had carried her Christmas groceries past the front-page *Times* photo in its vending machine window: an emaciated African child being whipped away from a food supply by a grown African man assigned to guard it.

There were only random incidents; encounters. When she ran before dawn, the town's homeless floated along the streets like B-movie zombies, from the armory where they were allowed to sleep on bitter nights. Jogging, she had come upon a tramp sitting at the sidewalk curb next to his battered metal walking brace; he had asked her at once, strickenly, *Will you help me?* He had fallen, and could not stand without assistance. He could have been crazy or held a knife but that caution only lasted a fraction of a second before she'd helped pull the man to standing—his grip on her forearm desperately strong, desperate to right and balance himself. She had tried not to notice his clothes, filthy and torn—got him situated, standing up again on the sidewalk, leaning on his brace. And then she'd had to run away, leaving him standing there alone on the sidewalk in the freezing dawn. And though he'd doubtless had some plan—if only to stagger in the direction of a smoke or a coffee—as she ran away from him the sobs bubbled erratically from deep in her like independent entities with minds quite their own. She had rarely run and wept at the same time: a queer business, but it could be done.

When she had said goodbye to Larry that night she had taken his hand, looked into his eyes and told him she hoped to see him for the same celebration next year. Oh God willing, he had answered, fixing her eyes with his own, imploring, grasping quick hold of her hand with both of his: the pressure instant and reflexive, a baby's hand automatically curling tight around the extended adult finger. As if he hoped he might receive a saving message, a vital grace osmosed through her hand into his. And it was clear to her then that a year more of any of this, on any terms, would be simply the best and dearest gift he could receive. *Christmas is a storm*, thought the woman. And we are hiding together, all of us, from the terror of seeing ourselves by lightning's light.

The Sounds That Arrive
in the Present

Belle hurt.

All over. Patches of her were staging, by turns in recent years, little insurrections. It was the time of life when all warranties ran out, and it was also the time when others were not interested to hear about the failures of your various parts. In fact it was a signal to folks, if you indulged in such descriptions, to back off a step or two—for them not to take you quite as seriously; to nod and smile and glance nervously around. So Belle mostly shut up, tried not to think about it, to dictate to herself that she could will the aches away.

First to march off the job was her skin. A lifetime lived in western sunlight now rewarded her with a number of precancerous eruptions, red places that periodically needed excising with surgical knives, then stitching up, then unguents for healing and unguents to protect against further damage—and now her face bears a network of tiny whispers, scars that the clever dermatologist crafted to be as minimally visible as his extraordinarily paid skills might allow. Thank God Belle has good insurance. The dermatologist takes African safaris on vacation.

Then her gums unveiled their little surprise: a big hole growing where bone should be, between a molar and its moist pink packing, requiring upper and lower—what was it called—osseo something, osseo surgery, an ordeal she now holds in mind as she forces herself through twenty minutes of elaborate nightly cleanings, hauling out a basket of tiny instruments and brushes and rinses and fluoride paints designed to keep flesh and enamel fastened stably enough to eat without further, wretchedly painful interventions. She had swallowed so much Tylenol after the surgery her shit had turned black.

There followed the matter of the knees. Jogging had given way, heeding certain highly specific twinges, to something called speed walking, which in full throttle looked like a kind of Olympics marathon for adult victims of mongolism. *This is so much harder,* she would fume as she puffed along, elbows working, *than simple running.* Running was automatic as breathing. Running was sitting down in a train to watch the colorful scenery reel past. Speed walking meant holding yourself rigid in various awkward grips, making and obeying multiple commands: *Punch it. Stomach in. Breastbone up, shoulders down.* A forced military march in some ways, because any golden dreams that might laze up to the surface as she strode—musings about life and time—fled like frightened fish whenever the military conscience barked. Well, the reward was the breaking of a sweat, and a reasonably shapely rump. But from time to time her knees telegraphed their unease, a series of little stabbings. From time to time her hip sockets would also moan—apropos of nothing — from a place so deep it made her envision X rays of her skeletal self.

Swimming had been a refuge until her arm rebelled. Rotator cuff strain, or so the physical therapist called it. They had names for everything, but they didn't have quick ways of fixing what they named. Repetitive stress syndrome, from computering too many years at her job. Belle did what millions of women did for a job. She sat at a desk, answered phones, typed correspondence and memos. She administered. Ministered, more like. Changed toilet paper rolls and shook hands with fire inspectors. Then she came home and ministered some more, to her husband Gene, her cheerful twelve-year-old Petey—reports on space debris or mountain lions, or the elaborate genealogy of Animorph characters. There were library books to recycle, cards and gifts to render, objects to grasp and carry and redeposit at their proper stations. What did it mean if most of your waking home life for the past dozen years had been spent washing and rinsing dishes and glasses? Was there a stunning secret in the crockery and glass that would yield itself up with enough rubbing, like a genie from a lamp? And morning and night, the imploring phone calls. Friends. Relatives. She could hear them inhaling to settle into it: a long, chewy chat. The phone rang insistently, like the hotline to a newsroom.

Oh, Belle was very tired.

And she hurt.

She would ask Gene to massage her after dinner, scrunching down between his knees where he sat on the couch, and he would give her neck and shoulders a few squeezes and pushes. Then he'd sort of pat her amicably and turn back toward the program he was watching about making tapenade, or the article on amortization. Gene was a postman. Affable and quiet, on his feet all day, he also cooked and did a great deal for the household; their two incomes together just squeakily enough to tie up the package of their combined lives—and he, too, was tired. She couldn't not love his freckles and wavy copper hair, his innovative repairs and flowerpots, his tolerant smile—always so patiently amused. But he hadn't much patience for back rubs. And Belle couldn't afford private masseurs.

So the physical therapy, when it became authorized by the young, weary Filipino doctor in town she had seen (who patted her on the back as he saw her out, as if she were imagining the shriek of pain in her shoulder that shot straight down to the top of her hand)—the therapy sessions were the one thing Belle looked forward to each week.

She would drive there from her office at five, so vacant with fatigue she nearly always missed the turn into the suburban parking lot. She would turn off the engine and in those strange moments of stark, silent, exhausted clarity that confront adults after turning off a car engine, she would sit quite still, staring at the afternoon light glinting hard off heedless traffic, the thin sad stripling trees surrounding the lot, drooping in relentless gusts of carbon monoxide. She would think, idly, about the facts of her present age: her listlessness, the bit of belly rounding over the C-section scar above her pubis no matter how many sit-ups she struggled through. Suburban, strapped into an eight-to-five, paying off a credit card and a mortgage—all the straits she had ferociously sworn at seventeen to abjure. The things Belle could name now that had been good—that appeared from this distance to have been unqualified good—jazz clubs, lovers, swimming in Polynesian freshwater pools or listening to the bells of the Pantheon at six o'clock on a swirling-snowy Paris evening—these experiences seemed to have shrunk on their own to small pebbles that rolled under the bulky furniture of her ongoing days. Belle pulled her eyes from the middle distance to glance over to her briefcase on the passenger seat, wondering whether to bring in the light paperback she always carried, which she read in furtive clusters of paragraphs at lunch hour. Then she would sigh and reach just for her wallet, knowing she could scarcely leaf through waiting-room magazines.

"And what is the state of our state?" Rae would ask once they were inside the little white treatment room—garish white fluorescents above tall white shelves crammed with white equipment—white jars of creams, white towels, a cushioned table with a clean piece of paper laid lengthwise. Rae would search Belle's face as she listened, her dark brown eyes so kind that Belle's impulse was to let tears flood forward. She checked the impulse, knowing Rae would already have read and heard and noted everything: the sigh of lost ideas, the pale skin, reddened eyes, the balled fist of exhaustion in her face.

Rae was lovely. Belle had thought so from their first handshake. She was small, delicate but sturdy, short haircut like a boy's, a shy, friendly, soft face and manner. Belle wondered whether Rae had a lover, and if she did, whether that might be a man or a woman. But something told Belle it was not for her to know, and Rae made no allusions. This avoidance made a certain gap in their talk, yet the two women immediately had an ease. At first not quite so much so as later. Because Belle hurt.

"I can't pull off a shirt," she had explained. Couldn't pour from a teakettle, or reach to a high shelf. Yanking the seat belt over her lap to snap into its lock made her grimace in anguish. Suddenly the arm was a lunatic child that refused to cooperate, screaming at each most mundane motion. Standing stripped in front of the bathroom mirror, pressing her two hands together before her in a prayerlike arrow, Belle saw her right shoulder sitting wrongly, much higher than her left, and that scared her enough to send her to the telephone.

Rae listened softly. *Yes. Softly,* thought Belle. She asked Belle that first session to mark a crude drawing of a human body showing where it hurt most and to report what level of pain: the chart's choices on each end of a little spectrum-bar were *mildly uncomfortable* and *most unbearable pain imaginable.* Belle thought briefly about these designations, and how, like small children, American people did their best to answer such commands precisely, accurately: as if perfect help would issue directly from their patient pencil marks. Belle supposed those people on the unbearable end would receive drugs of some sort. *Well,* she thought. *Doesn't really fix anything.*

"I think I know exactly what is going on," said Rae finally, whose eyes had never left Belle's face, watching with such keenness it seemed to Belle as if Rae were reading subtitles that ran invisibly beneath Belle's spoken words. She showed Belle a detailed anatomical map and pointed to the areas Belle had marked. Belle listened as Rae told her about exercises she had to do, and ultrasound treatments, and low electric currents they'd run, with little stickers, into her shoulders and upper back. But very best, each session, was when Rae dragged in a strange chair that looked like a device for obscure sexual gymnastics. You kneeled and fit your face in a padded hole like a catcher's mitt, your arms resting on padding to either side. Your whole weight could relax forward. Rae would put cream on her hands and massage Belle's knotted back and shoulders.

At the touch of Rae's hands, Belle always wanted to weep. So sore she could scarcely care about the question that hummed dully at a muffled distance from Rae's chatting voice: *How had she come to live this way?* Every step had made sense as she'd taken it. Fall in love with the man. Welcome the child. Take the nearby job, a decent second income. But now she felt squashed by the equation's simple total. Needed money, needed family: No exit. Body in serious rebellion. You washed the dishes and cleaned your teeth, read a sentence or two from a magazine and picked up the same routines early next morning. You packed everyone's lunch, filled the car with gas, bought groceries, laundered, scrubbed and swept and set the clock. There were second and third worlds where mortal safety was never assumed and such comforts as Belle's were unspeakably luxurious, but it did not change the facts of her aching, her stupor, and this confounded her. It wasn't fair to compare yourself with a pack animal, or one of those mules that goes in eternal circles, tied to a lever that turns a pump. But of course she did.

Belle fancied she could almost hear Rae thinking. Probably, Rae was prohibited from pushing patients too hard to change their lives. But she could hint.

She did it so gently.

"How can we get rid of some of that stress?" Rae murmured as she worked the taut wires and ridges of Belle's freckled back, a back Belle had always felt grateful for. It was symmetrical and strong, covered with a constellation of freckles in virtually a replicate pattern of her late father's, a big man whose body had seemed a hearth of safety. Nothing at all had been safe, of course; he had died young, of drink and rich food. But when she was little he had loomed, and she still keeps a photograph of her infant self peering over his youthful bare back, chubby fists grasping a broad freckled shoulder, her squint that of a mildly amazed guest in the vast palace of the world.

Her own back had lasted her all this time, apart from a couple of minor strains. It had swum with her and run with her (even barefoot, on beaches and in parks), and lately it speed walked. It stretched and twisted and rebounded from loads she should never have lifted. But now her shoulders were complaining. Their speech was voluble. They wanted to retire. They wanted to sleep until eight, have a stretch and a swim, later a nice nap. They did not want their owner to bother with heels and hose. They wanted quietude, rest, cushiony sandals, plenty of salad and fresh fruit and clean air.

Belle was nowhere near being able to retire.

At Rae's kind question Belle was flummoxed, too tired to think properly; the question made her as tired as the pain that prompted the question. Belle swallowed a bowlful of vitamins nightly. She tried to have lights out by eleven, though it probably should have been ten. Money was the reason, of course. Money was everyone's reason. A dreary, stupid, necessary reason and it shamed her to have fallen into the great grainy swill of middle-aged adults caught in numbing rounds because of need for some niggling, pathetic salary. She felt like a figurine on one of those old European tower clocks, the carved-wood peasants that banged out of little double doors at the advent of each hour, little mallets raised above their heads, striking the visible bells or one another, turning and whirring back along the track through their doors.

A notion scratched faintly offstage of Belle's thinking: There was something she was forgetting, that she had been supposed to do. Something she had forgotten all her life to do, and would only remember—with a spreading heat of insane horror—when it was too late.

She had the distinct sense it was something very simple. Something important, something that had been right in front of her to do the whole time. But it swam from her focus each time she felt it close, like a mark the eyeball tries to study on its own lubricated surface.

Rae was pressing deeply into something about the size of a large marble, midway down Belle's spine, slightly to the right. It sent out deep shock waves of pain, like an electric siren. Belle felt a nauseating tingling shoot down to her toes. She gasped, and something between her ears briefly entertained the option of fainting.

"That . . . is . . . very bad," she panted.

"Mmm. Trying to work some of these out," soothed Rae. During the last part of the sessions, when Rae would turn the timer for a quarter-hour and leave Belle laying quietly on the table under a weighted heating pad, dimming the lights before she left the room—that was when Belle could not think of one single other thing she truly, actively wanted, except to be left warm and snugly wrapped here in this room and forgotten. Forgotten by all living beings who currently asked anything of her existence. Her existence! Frayed old scrap, wadded up and stuffed into this neutral cramped room with its mute nonjudging creams and towels and machinery: clean, square, white, windowless, silent; bland enough to cancel memory and desire, depth and texture—room with no past and no future, only a few faded floral watercolors on the walls, so bleached away as to nearly be gone. A room that knew nothing.

Belle herself wanted to go away. She wanted not to be. Not who she was now, anyway, nor where, nor what—a bland, frayed old hurting scrap. Something she'd thought could never, ever happen. And now that it had, what most stung her was the utter commonness of it: the astonishing fact that even though it was her all this was happening to, it was bitterly uninteresting.

"Rae, where are you from?" Belle wanted a door to step through. She wanted to lift up a corner of the roof and climb out, like the foolish wanderer in the tarot card illustration she had once carried around and pasted up in every room she rented as a young adventuress: a prop, part of the portable shrine, along with her Rilke and Salinger, her guitar and typewriter. She must have bought that poster at the Renaissance Pleasure Faire, the time the big papier-mâché giant on stilts had thought her sexy and made a beeline for her, giving her such a fright she had hidden behind the Drumsticke and Meade stand. The Fool in the poster picture was actually peeling up a corner of his home's roof like the crust of a pie—or wait, was he lifting away a piece of the visible sky, like an attic trapdoor?—maybe that was it. And found himself gaping at the wide, brilliant cosmos behind the sky, all manner of planets and stars moving, ticking, radiant and graceful, intricately coordinated above his gaze like a burnished heavenly watchworks. He had been smiling, that Fool, rapt and awed and gratified in that painting.

"Pacific Northwest," answered Rae, with little inflection.

Belle saw it at once: raw, wet country, dripping and rocky, cold rain, high clouds that moved constantly, cold ocean, pungent tall firs. "Beautiful?"

"Oh yes," murmured the voice above the hands that pressed into neck and upper arms and that triangle of shoulder blades in the back, where wings would be if we were angels.

"When did you live there, Rae? What did you do?"

"I lived on an island. I was very young." It seemed to Belle that though her bare back was facing Rae, she could hear Rae smiling a little.

"Really? With who—ah, whom?" The reflex honed by homework.

"Alone."

A beat.

"By yourself? On an entire island?"

Rae had been merely seventeen years old when she decided to live out her fantasy. She packed up and set off against her parents' wishes, making camp on one of a small clutch of tiny islands off the Gulf Islands of Canada, north of the San Juans. She'd got permission to squat there from the island's owner—it was a small bit of land, a few acres, fairly flat except for some rises and outcroppings of giant boulder. In the midst of a stand of laurels Rae assembled the driftwood boards and nails she'd collected, and a real door she'd found from an abandoned shack someone had fashioned years earlier. Rae built herself a little structure there, with windows (canvas tarps over them), and a skylight over her bed. She had everything she needed—Coleman stove, simple bed, pots, plates, and so on. She dug a very admirable latrine, at the regulation distance and depth, and used ash instead of lye. She made a run across the mile-wide bay in her outboard canoe once a week to the nearest town for supplies and drinking water. Rae loved her isolated life. She read books, tried to meditate, took long walks. When it rained—which was often, a soft, steady rain—she caught the leaks in pans, read, wrote and sketched in a journal, did crosswords, napped, lit candles, practiced the flute. Rae loved her island, the stillness of the rocks and trees, smells of conifers and laurel. She had a favorite little dog with her, Icarus: a part-golden lab with a bum leg, who kept her pleasant company.

Belle tried to turn her head sideways a moment. "Did you see other people at all?"

"A few, sometimes. There were others who had similar camps going, on little islands near to mine," Rae said. They were about a mile of water apart from each other. Everyone had a small motorboat to get around in. "We were all young," Rae said.

"Yes," Belle sighed, plopping her face forward into its padded hole. She remembered a two-level tepee on a Hawaiian island, way up on the grassy heights of the dormant volcano, looking down into the lights of the tiny town below. All they'd had for entertainment at night was a portable radio, which they tuned to the local Japanese station, and listened to its lovesick dedication—"for Joyce, from Sherman: three little words"—then the music: musty old songs like "I'm Mr. Blue" and "Raindrops," while they played cribbage. At night it smelled pure as a clean baby up there, the moon gliding in and out of spun clouds, playing over the tiny ripples of the sea. They slept in down bags and ate vegetarian dinners from the garden just outside, sometimes having to pick a fat worm from the broccoli. Belle would not want to be living there again; true. But she could enter the field of mind that seemed to be driving things then, at least if she concentrated. It was a field that opened out and out, without your being able to see or even guess where it might wind up.

"There was a boating accident," Rae was saying.

Belle came to in a delayed beat. "Accident? What do you mean?"

There were others, as Rae had mentioned, who'd set up little homestead camps on the smaller islands scattered in the inlet.

One was a fisherman, one was a writer; there was a couple who were traveling and adventuring. From time to time they gave parties for each other. The way they got across the water's distance to each other, perhaps a mile, were these motorboats, crude when Rae now considers it—the kind you see fishermen trolling in; not much more to them than Tom Sawyer's raft with a motor, she supposed. And one night after celebrating and drinking too much, a passel of these young people had boarded a fourteen-foot fiberglass boat with the intention of going to visit someone else's island. Rae wore a sweatshirt and a long skirt and boots and brought her mandolin.

They were living a Peter Pan dream, thought Belle. *The lost boys and their Wendys.* Belle saw in her mind a little archipelago of forts and campsites. How we did think nothing of such things then, she reminded herself. We hiked into the volcanic crater, seven miles down gravel switchback paths, by moonlight. We stood naked at the cliff's edge in the pounding wind. It was what you did.

Rae continued to speak quietly. It was February, she said, and the water very cold, going deep immediately once offshore. The group had been drinking, and the boat's owner made a grave error in judgment. Seven people, including Rae and Rae's dog, had boarded the motorboat without life jackets, and the craft was making its way with a lawn-mower buzz in the direction of the neighboring island. So many stars were out, Rae said. The stars were close and brilliant; their light glittered on the cold black water of the Northwest sound. That was when Rae became mesmerized by the phosphorus.

The phosphorescent cells glowed wherever the water was disturbed: Rae could not take her eyes off the boat's wake, which seemed lit from within by a holy silver-blue as the craft plowed ahead. The entire wake of the boat and surrounding water ran like molten silver, as if singled out by an otherworldly attention—liquid mercury peeling open. Rae stared at the gilt water and the thought came quite clearly: *If I were to die tonight, on such a beautiful night, it would be okay.*

The boat had got a mile offshore, its intoxicated young pas-sengers talking and laughing. But Rae could not take her eyes from the mystical sight of the luminous liquid-mercury wake. And then somehow she also noticed that the silver lines were streaming, in rhythmic little surges, over the sides of the boat. The boat had begun taking on water. The weight of the seven was too much: far too much for the fragile craft. Rae yelled to the driver to slow down, that they were taking on water. He did. And the instant he did the boat's entire wake flooded the craft, one fast-forward motion before their dumb, incredulous eyes. The young friends screamed at each other, but no one could stop what was happening. That was the singular thing, and after nearly twenty years Rae still thinks about how fast it happened. Faster than anyone could notice a beginning, it had ended. Suddenly the entire band of them were treading freezing water, screaming at each other in the 45-degree sea. Two of Rae's friends on this voyage were engaged to be married. When the boat was completely gone the young man of the couple, Rick, screamed, *I can't swim, man*—but it was only Rae who heard him in the din.

She looked toward Rick in the water and his arms were waving in a circle. He wore a leather jacket with fringe. Rae started automatically to swim toward him but in the same moment thought, *Where am I going to take him.* The boat was down. There was nothing to hold. Panic and screaming and people flailing in freezing water who could scarcely breathe. Rae shrieked to the unheeding others to save him. She looked toward him again— and this time there was only quiet water where his arms had been.

Belle's breath seemed stuck in her thorax. "My God." It was a secret terror of hers—death by drowning. Water filling lungs without pity, without cessation, precious air withheld, panic and pain and blackness of no-air. The once-beautiful stars bearing down, zooming in on you like a devil's trick, a fiend's smile, a grinning mouthful of gleaming teeth: *Your last night, your last breath and you didn't know it, couldn't know that this was to be it this is it Oh God*— Yet here was Rae, standing behind her, murmuring, hands rhythmic on her shoulders, speaking softly to her.

Belle's breath had halted. "What—what did you do."

Rae had ripped her long skirt and kicked off her boots in order to be able to swim better. Her dog had swum directly for her
in his fright, but she had had to push him violently away, or he
would have drowned them both. He swam off.

Belle's breath still felt paralyzed, high in her chest. Her voice
came like a child's. "What did you decide—how did you—"

"I wanted to swim back," Rae answered, still working Belle's
spine, placid, contained, calm as all the normal words she had
ever spoken since Belle had met her. "And I started to. But the
others yelled that I would be crazy to do that, that it would finish me off, and that our only hope was to stay together and yell
for help." The boat's very tip had bobbed back up, perhaps with
some air still under it. They clung. They counted, and they yelled.

Belle saw the black, star-covered water, chopping and flickering around the panting, paddling, terrified group. Black ice soup,
the planet's blood, indifferent, cruelly beautiful, more of it than
anything else, heedless, ready to take them into itself as easily as
rain.

"We counted to ten and yelled *help* with all our might," Rae
said, pressing her thumbs warmly into the small of Belle's waist.
The fact of what Rae was doing—her reflective voice from this long
safe distance, massaging Belle in her physical therapy uniform,
inside the white walls of this dry, bland, indifferent room—
alongside the events she was describing—stunned Belle's mind
like a snakebite.

"What . . . happened?" Belle's voice cracked midway, laryngi-
tis-style.

"Someone finally came out to us in another boat," mused Rae.
"They heard us from the other side of the island. They thought
our motor had died, and they heard us. They came out in a big-
ger boat and gathered us on. When they hauled me in I landed
upside-down in the boat on my head, and I found I could not
move. I could not move my legs or feet. The others, too."

The group's rescuers took them back and stripped them and
wrapped them in all the blankets they could find, sat them in
front of the fire they'd built. No one could stop shaking, as hard
a shaking, Rae said, as she had ever known or seen: like one of

those machines that shakes paint. For hours. They had hypothermia.

"We were in shock," Rae added after a moment, almost bashfully.

"Rae!" Belle breathed.

"And then, the most wonderful thing," Rae laughed, a rueful single cluck, as if to herself now. "My little dog, Icarus. Found me. Came running to me."

He had swum, with his bad leg, all the way back to the island.

Belle felt, in the next moment, that that rueful cluck had in fact been Rae's voice breaking, just the slightest hair. She did not dare turn around. Rae said nothing for a long time, and then Belle thought she heard the smallest intake and exhale of wet air.

The survivors huddled around the fire the rest of that night, dozing in pained spurts of what sleep might come, still shaking, still wrapped in scratchy wool blankets with holes in them. Next day the exhausted young people made their way to Salt Spring Island to report the accident, and the death of their friend, to the Royal Canadian Mounted Police. No charges were brought. The Coast Guard searched for Rick's body for days, as did his family from Ottawa, and his fiancée. It was never found.

Belle had nowhere to place her incredulity. Any gesture, any common expression of shock of sympathy or horror would have just then been gross, a polluting insult to Rae's quiet bearing. Belle struggled with the visions of the events now jumbling together in her mind's eye, a pile of haunted photographs. There was some terrible, sweet comprehension in Rae's telling. And somehow, it shamed Belle.

"Rae. Do you still—can you ever again face—"

"Water? Yes, oh yes. I went kayaking a while after. I couldn't turn away from that part of things, and—well, remember—I was young."

After Belle had used up her allotted sessions with the physical therapy office, she took herself back swimming at the municipal pool.

It hurt at first. Her arm didn't want to, and it ached a long time after. But Belle pressed ahead with it, inventing a sort of lame crawl stroke, alternating that with a spastic backstroke. She'd take herself at the end of the workday when few others were around and everything above ground and below water was turning teal blue. She lowered herself into the warmish pool and pushed off, using the hurting arm in a folded-up way. Looking up at the limitless blue-going-to-indigo, she'd paddle back and forth. When the moon and a sprinkle of stars rose early they would break up in her vision as her face lifted and immersed in the water, so that splashes of milk sparkled over her glimpses of where she was going. And slowly, slowly, her arm unfolded.

Belle can swim a mile now. She called Rae once or twice, to tell her.

At about the same time, Belle taught herself another habit.

A secret one.

She drives on her lunch break to the shadows of an old neighborhood in the little farm town near her office. Trees are tall there and the wind sings through them. Everybody seems away at that hour, to work or school, or maybe asleep. Belle parks in the deepest shade by a big wall of bushes, and turns off the car.

She opens all the windows, climbs into the backseat and reclines out of sight against a pillow. It is a scruffy neighborhood of weather-softened farmhouses and long cool grass. Pines live intimately with oaks and birch and eucalyptus, all of them very tall. No one's around.

Belle watches, and listens.

She can hear a wind chime's occasional *chang,* like a cowbell. A lone bee makes the rounds. Finches dart, very small with chartreuse chests and tiny peeps that sound like *squirt, squirt.* A dove's cry, distant. A crow's, claiming territory. Scents of grass, of jasmine, of pine. Belle looks attentively: A yucca plant. Brilliant orange poppies. A fat dragonfly. Jays and robins. Someone hammering in a yard. The wind, a rushing overture, and Belle can lean back and see out the open windows a wide rippling fabric of loosely stitched birch leaves reflecting in the afternoon sky like turning coins, green-silver-green.

All that matters then is being quiet, and picking out as many sounds as she can. Remnants of sounds may come to her in her head, too, besides the ones going on right there. Choruses of famous music, carousel organs, *thunking* of waves on beaches, sirens in cities, shouts from playgrounds. Scraps of people's voices: her father's, her mother's, adults and children from years ago—like turning a radio dial and sliding over random blurts of phrases and tunes and sentences. All of it seems to blend together with the sounds that arrive in the present—the distant plane's drone, someone's old wood saw, the dog barking down the street, even a rooster announcing itself somewhere. Especially, though, the wind. Belle looks up through the car's rear window for a perfect view: the giant trees' interlocking leaves glow like clear lime candies with the sun pouring through the backs of them, and they begin to stir with the wind. The wind is a silken quilt over the whole of it, the voice over all the other voices. Everything came down to this, and that was the thing of it. This was what the dead listened to.

If she concentrates and trains her ears hard to it, Belle can finally hear the soft, far roar of the whole muted world going about its frantic day. Once she can make it out, that vibrating wash of white noise is curiously familiar. Yes, she had heard it long before; identified it without fear when she was a little girl walking home from school under an infinite white sky of late afternoon. Belle remembers, in something like a rolling spasm of sweet completeness, that she had only calmly wondered then, as a child, what shape it would take and how it would feel— that roar of simultaneous life in the waiting world, when she entered it.

About the Author

Photo by Jeanette Vonier

Joan Frank was born to New Yorkers in Phoenix, Arizona, and has lived in the Hawaiian Islands and San Francisco. Her literary nonfiction and short stories have appeared in *The Iowa Review, American Literary Review, Confrontation, Salmagundi, Notre Dame Review, Antioch Review,* and many other anthologies and journals. She is a MacDowell Colony Fellow, Pushcart Prize nominee, and winner of the Iowa Literary Award for short fiction. She has taught the short story at San Francisco State University and is currently working on a new collection of stories and a book about the writing life. She lives in Santa Rosa, California, with playwright Robert Duxbury.